Dry Milk

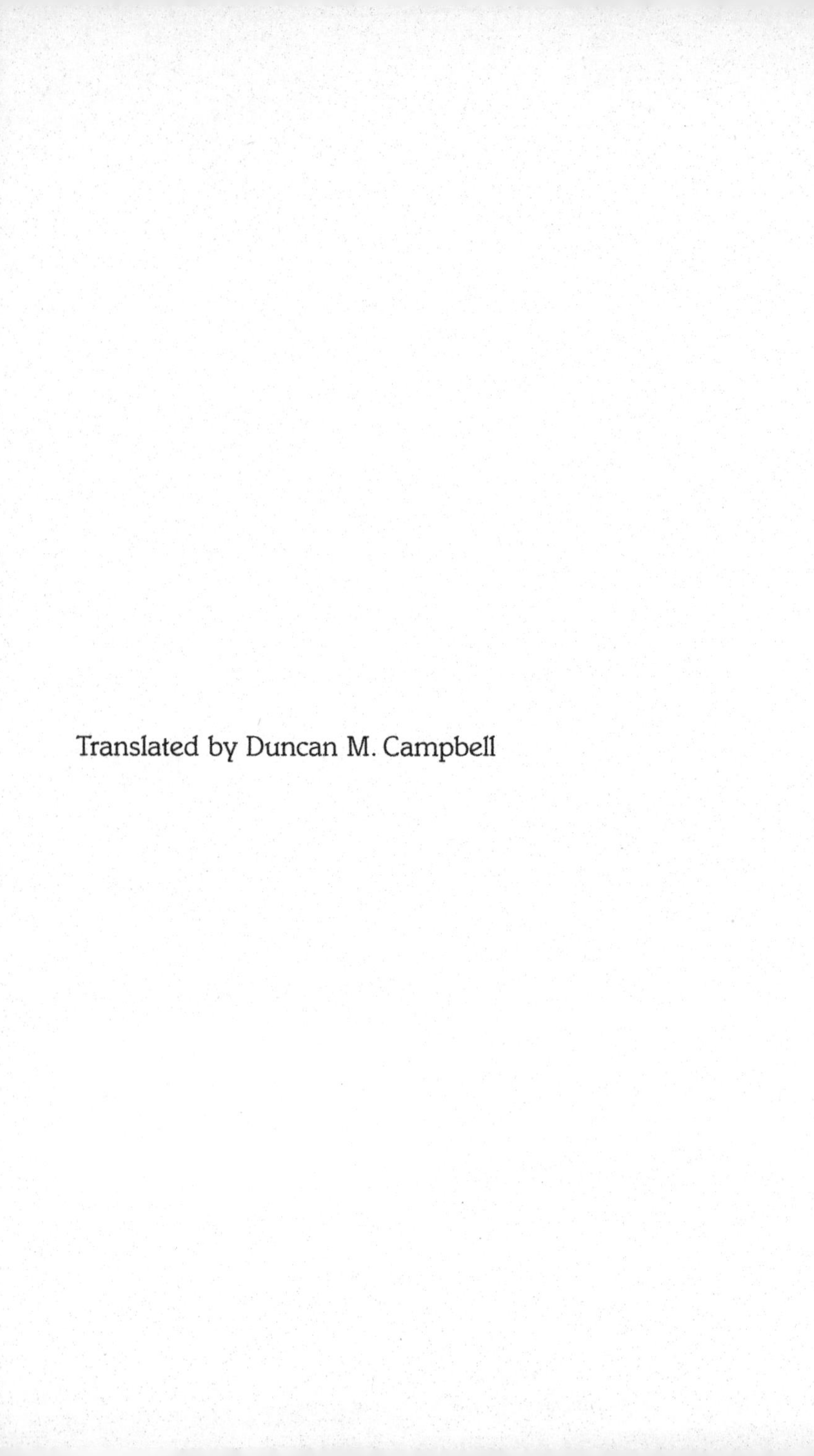

Translated by Duncan M. Campbell

Huo Yan

Dry Milk

GIRAMONDO

Published in 2019
from the Writing and Society Research Centre
at Western Sydney University
by the Giramondo Publishing Company
PO Box 752
Artarmon NSW 1570 Australia
www.giramondopublishing.com

First published in China in *Shanhua* 2013
Under the title *Li Yuehan*

Designed by Harry Williamson
Typeset by Andrew Davies
in 11.25/15 pt Garamond 3

Printed and bound by Ligare Book Printers
Distributed in Australia by NewSouth Books

A catalogue record for this
book is available from the
National Library of Australia

ISBN: 978-1-925336-99-3

9 8 7 6 5 4 3 2 1

Dry Milk

It was thirty years to the day since John Lee had first arrived in New Zealand. He thought he might shut up shop early to mark the anniversary.

Just as his last would-be customer was about to enter the shop, he flipped over the sign in the front window to read CLOSED. Having beaten the customer to the door by a pace or two, John Lee locked it and ducked back out of sight. Lifting a corner of the blind, he watched as the man knocked agitatedly on the door as he peered into the shop, pressing his face hard against the glass pane so that it resembled an egg stuck to a wok, distorted beyond recognition. The man stayed this way for quite some time before he wandered off, swearing loudly.

From his hiding place, John Lee let out a laugh – a

strange sound, forced out through throat and nose. He congratulated himself on having made the right decision. Those Islanders would forever wander aimlessly around his shop, only to pick up some item or another and try to bargain with him over its price. Meanwhile, their fat arses would bump over the displays of goods as they wandered down the aisles. Everything seemed strange and new to them, and whilst they never really intended to buy anything, the burnt-toffee colour of their skins would soil everything they happened to pick up.

John Lee cast a glance at the clock hanging from the clothes rack. Half past five. He would wait another half an hour, he decided. Come six p.m., the supermarkets started putting reduced-price stickers on all their fresh produce. He was going to have a big meal tonight, in celebration.

As if she knew what was going through his mind, the woman began to salivate, drops falling from the corner of her mouth onto the wooden table he had just acquired.

'Hungry? We'll have a feast tonight.' John Lee wiped away the saliva with his sleeve and patted her on the shoulder, his eyes fixed all the while on the ivory-coloured face of the plastic clock. As if speaking to himself, he continued: 'Thirty years. How quickly they've passed.'

As soon as six came around, John Lee locked the door of the shop and took out the keys to his car. It was a battered old Charade, bought second-hand, its body painted a grassy green colour. The car's doors, which had to be unlocked by hand, were marked with a silver stripe. The vehicle sat so close to the ground that anyone of normal size had to bend low to get into it; John Lee pressed down hard on the woman's head to get her into her seat. Squashed into the car with her legs bunched up under her chin, she looked most uncomfortable.

John Lee helped her fasten her seatbelt, making sure she was well secured. Going around to the driver's side of the car, he got in himself, taking a quick glance in the rear-view mirror at his HI JOHN baseball cap. It was a hat he wore all day every day, taking it off only when he went to bed. His spare grey hair poked out around its edges.

In the supermarket the shop assistants were busy changing the price labels. John Lee shopped strictly according to price, always carefully comparing the price of every item as he placed it in his shopping trolley. He noticed several Islanders ogling items in the meat aisle, and then sweeping up the trays of beefsteak on special and putting them in their shopping baskets. John Lee panicked, knowing that if he didn't act quickly they would lay their hands on all the cut-price meat, and his celebratory banquet would disappear down their throats rather than his.

He grabbed several packets of beefsteak and thrust them into the woman's hands. She hugged them to her breast, grinning at the Islanders, exposing the yellow flesh between her teeth. John Lee hated it when she smiled; her rotting teeth offered proof that she never remembered to brush them. He pulled her aside, hiding her behind him, his attention soon enough captured again by his quest for food. He grabbed the items he needed, shaking the packets determinedly before putting them down and selecting another. He was only ever satisfied when he managed to buy the cheapest products on sale.

All the cashiers had Asian faces. He picked the most Chinese-looking girl.

'Hello,' he said in Mandarin.

The cashier smiled and replied, in English: 'Hello.'

Unsure whether or not she had understood him, he tried again to address her in Mandarin.

The girl swiped the items one by one as if she hadn't heard him, her faced fixed in a polite smile. '$68.90,' she announced in perfect English.

The amount took John Lee by surprise. It was far more than he had anticipated. In English, he asked her to double-check the price of each of the items he had placed in his trolley. Behind him, a queue had formed, but the cashier patiently helped him go through the receipt item by item, and he realised that neither of the two packets of beefsteak he had grabbed had 'special' stickers attached to them. Both were sirloin steaks of the finest quality.

For a moment he stood rooted to the spot.

'Okay,' he said. 'Could you put the two packets of meat in separate bags, and can you let me have two rubbish bags as well?'

John Lee took as long as he could over paying, as if to slow down the speed with which the money left his pocket. He took three twenty-dollar notes from his calf-leather wallet: three waterproof notes that made no sound as they were being counted. Then, with a dull crash, he emptied out his loose change on the checkout counter. With the checkout girl, he counted the coins one by one until they reached the required amount. Some of the expectations he'd had for his banquet began to return. The amount he had paid for his groceries was enough to pay for a good meal at a Chinese restaurant. He experienced a slight surge of satisfaction as he departed the supermarket without so much as a 'thank you' to the cashier, having thrown a glare in the direction of the Islanders queued up behind him.

His house was a short drive away. After going around a corner or two, John Lee parked the car halfway up the slope of the hill where their house was the only one. It was an old house, built over a hundred years earlier.

Having parked, he opened the boot of the car and took out the three plastic bags of shopping, placing them on the golden leaves that littered the pavement. Only once he had done so did he tell the woman to get out of the car, locking the doors and yanking on the handles repeatedly to be sure they couldn't be opened.

The house was like a small warehouse, crammed with things he had scavenged from around the place. A health inspector had called by once, pointing out to him how easily a house such as this could catch fire. He'd paid the warning no heed, telling her that he didn't smoke, that there were no open fireplaces in the house, and that soon enough everything he had piled up there would be taken to his shop to be sold. As he said this, he had cast the softly spoken inspector, whose name was Lucy, a look that implied: 'This is my business. Nothing to do with you.' She stood up and straightened the pleats on her skirt. 'In that case, Mr Lee, I'll be going. I hope you have a good day.'

Mumbling to himself in Mandarin, John Lee saw her out: 'I'd be a lot happier if you lot would just pay out more in welfare benefits and bother less with finding fault with everyone else.'

Lucy frowned, and shook his hand in farewell, before getting into her little Mercedes-Benz.

Later on, at a Chinese community reception, he happened to encounter her again. She was speaking with the staff of the Chinese Consulate in fluent Mandarin. Looking in his direction, she raised her wine glass to him, the glass refracting the hint of a smile that remained on her face for a moment.

John Lee's kitchen window looked out over the seashore. Between the shore and the house lay a neglected garden in the midst of which stood, among a mass of vegetation, a wooden sign with the year carved into it. The scene gave him some sense of satisfaction, though if someone were to offer him money to renovate he would no doubt have felt better about his lot in life. The fact that the woman was an imbecile served to make his sense of grievance pointless, and so all he did was complain endlessly about the weather.

To do justice to the sirloin, John Lee decided to try to cook a Western meal. For the past thirty years, he had stuck with Chinese cooking. The woman had no interest whatsoever in food as long as she could fill her belly. For a long time he had taken pains over the cooking, but now he had lost interest and his efforts often amounted merely to buying readymade meals from the supermarket that appealled only to Chinese workers.

John Lee marinated the meat for a while, sprinkling it with a mix of sauces. A previous tenant had left the condiments behind when they moved out; John Lee had fished them out of the rubbish bin and lined them up in the kitchen cupboard.

The house had three bedrooms. John Lee and the woman slept in the largest of these, with the other two let out to international students. Since the departure of his last tenant, both rooms had stood empty for six months, reducing his income by a good two thousand dollars a month. For this entire period, he had not once offered her even a smile; nobody, it seemed, was willing to live with an imbecile.

John Lee had cut off the house's internet connection and locked the rooms, fearing the woman would make a mess of them. She had taken to peeling the wallpaper with her fingers and throwing the pieces over herself, like confetti, an act she had learned from a television program in which a flower girl scattered petals over a bride. Since then, envious, she had been scratching at the wallpaper. Time and again, John Lee had been forced to stop her from swallowing pieces of wallpaper. He tried painting the rooms, but then he ran out of the light-green paint he had been using, and left the bedrooms as they were. The woman ignored the painted green walls completely, and then, before long, forgot her confetti obsession altogether.

Dressed in an apron, John Lee felt himself ridiculous. Thirty years ago, he had gone to visit his relatives, one by one, slapping his passport down on the table for them to see. 'Take a look,' he had said. 'I'm leaving.' The ambition that drove him on then had by now disappeared completely, as if doused in cold water.

He placed the marinated steak in the oven and set the dial to 'economical roast'. He stir-fried several dishes of cheap vegetables, bought just before the grocery stalls shut up shop. John Lee would snort with contempt whenever he saw vegetables being sold at full price.

John Lee shut the woman in the house all day watching television, never allowing her to go out of her own accord. She would tiptoe about without making a sound, always seeming as if she were about to creep up on him and try to scare him. She would squat on a stool watching historical operas on the Chinese channel, wearing a raffia cape around her shoulders that he had picked up second-hand, as if she were trying to imitate the swirling sleeves of the imperial concubines she was watching. Through the kitchen door, the continuous swish-swishing of the cape set his mind at ease.

Thirty minutes passed before he dared to take the steak out of the oven. He never ate anything that hadn't been thoroughly cooked; only barbarians ate food that was raw or cold. The juices that had seeped from the steak sizzled in the tinfoil. His gloved right hand slipped a bit as he took the steak out, and the oven tray splattered juice over the glove. With his left hand he quickly tried to brush it off, and in so doing grazed the tray. He pulled his bare hand back in a flash, letting out a groan at his scalded finger.

He swore and ran the cold tap, putting his hand under the water as a translucent white blister began to rise on the finger. He sucked in a deep breath, attempting to settle himself.

Even the slightest sense of celebration was gone. Outside the day had turned grey and there was a feeling of rain in the air. The leaves in the trees rustled in the wind and began to fall to the ground.

'Its about to rain again,' he thought. He hated the rain. This winter it had rained for more than a week nonstop and he had started to feel unwell, his body cold and dry but his face always clammy. Along with the sound of wind and rain, an overwhelming sense of loneliness had infiltrated his life.

He opened the door into the sitting room and called out for the woman to join him, and soon the two of them sat face to face across the long thin wooden table. The furniture in the house was old and gave off a smell of mildew, but, after thirty years here, that smell brought a small sense of comfort to him.

John Lee thought for a moment. He still hadn't opened the bottle of red wine. He poured her a glass of juice and clinked glasses with her.

'Tonight we're celebrating. Thirty years.'

The woman had no head for numbers. She wore a high-necked red cardigan embroidered with a white cat with eyes made from black plastic beads, its colour worn and the beads hanging loosely off her front. She cut her steak laboriously, the sauce all the while dripping onto her clothes as she ate – but she didn't notice, and as she chewed a look of happiness spread across her face.

He resented how easily she found pleasure. But for his own impatient desire to change the circumstances of his life, he would never have married her. Their marriage had been the basis on which he had been granted the right to migrate to New Zealand. Her parents had been underground party members who, under attack during the Cultural Revolution, had gassed themselves in their apartment. Their daughter was the only member of the family who had been saved but the carbon dioxide had left her in her current state. Once the Cultural Revolution was over, it was discovered that she had distant relatives living in New Zealand, and a change in government policy dictated that she be sent overseas. Having heard rumours of this development, John Lee – Li Yong as he was then known – took himself off to see the official in charge of her fate.

'I'm willing to marry her. And look after her,' he had told him.

'You sure about this?'

'Yep,' he replied, staring at his feet as the sweat from his neck dripped onto the leather shoes he had borrowed for the occasion. He nodded slightly.

'According to due process, we need to solicit the views of all those concerned,' the official said, as he turned to look at the woman. 'Comrade Wang Lina, are you willing to become man and wife with Comrade Li Yong?'

Sitting on a stool in the corner, fiddling with the eyes of the cat on her brand new red cardigan, she had seemed to understand what she had been asked, for she had nodded her head vigorously.

John Lee's store was closed on Sundays. He had bought it, a second-hand shop filled with junk, a decade earlier. When he had first arrived in New Zealand he had tried his hand at a variety of jobs before he was finally able to become his own boss.

The shop was a small one, piled high with so many things that in order to pass down the aisle one had to turn sideways. John Lee would sit the woman at the counter. Whenever anyone turned up in the shop, she uttered a strange noise. New customers would be taken aback by the sound, but over time, they got used to it and would always buy something before they left. John Lee discovered that human kindness could be turned to commercial advantage. He placed a glass jar on the counter beside her and made up a sign that read: 'HELP THE MENTALLY DISABLED: PLEASE GIVE GENEROUSLY.' Taking out two crumpled ten-dollar notes from his pocket, he placed these in the jar, along with some coins. At the end of every day he would count the money in the jar, sometimes finding that as much as twenty dollars had been donated. At such times he would give the woman a peck on the cheek, as if to reward her, his dry lips brushing her withered skin.

As a result of a nightmare he had once had, John Lee made a point of driving past his shop every day of the week. In the dream, his shop had been sealed up with strips of paper written on in black ink. A crowd had gathered in front of the store and, when he pushed his way through the crowd and put his face hard up against the glass, the interior was in blackened chaos, as though a fire had passed through. He smashed the window with his fist and cut his arm, but in his dream he felt no pain. He shouted: 'I need to get in, I'm the owner of this shop.' All of a sudden, several powerfully built Islanders took him by the shoulders, shouting at him as they did so: 'We'll soon be in charge of the shop.' John Lee swore at them in Mandarin in the most obscene terms, but they seemed unmoved and shoved him out of the crowd. The Westerners standing around laughed, their faces exhibiting the uncaring expressions that had become so familiar to him.

His eyes had opened suddenly and he found the woman was lying on top of him, her face pressed close to his, her breath stale. The details of the nightmare flashed through his mind.

He rushed to the garage and started up his car. When he arrived at the shop, he discovered everything was safe and sound. It was a weekend and there weren't many people around. The sun shone brightly off the sign – SEA DRAGON ANTIQUE SHOP – blinding him for a moment through his tears.

On the first Sunday of every month, John Lee attended a meeting of the Chinese Community Hope Association, an organisation he had joined on the recommendation of Uncle Wang, who collected the goods he sold at his shop. Uncle Wang was a committee member of the association and he took every opportunity to recommend it to others within the Chinese community. It took some time before

John Lee realised that Uncle Wang's enthusiasm for the association was mostly aimed at giving more importance to his position on the committee.

The chairman of the association was Taiwanese. Word was that he had never married but that he lived with a Westerner. John Lee paid his behaviour close attention. Every now and then, unconsciously, he would seem to form with his hands the delicate 'orchid fingers' gestures of the Kunqu opera, and cast a seductive look around him. It was only later on that John Lee learned how, before Liberation, this Taiwanese man with the amorous voice had indeed been a famous opera singer.

The association would organise activities every Sunday. Ever since John Lee had cut off the internet, Uncle Wang had become his sole source of news, and at times would make a glowing recommendation of some local happening or other, only for John Lee to discover it was an event in which Uncle Wang played a vital role. John Lee didn't mind the duplicity; his relationship with Uncle Wang was a complicated one. If he relied upon him for news, he also took no pains to hide the dislike he felt towards him. Uncle Wang had arrived in New Zealand five years earlier with his daughter, who had come as an international student, and he had only recently been granted permanent residency, one step short of citizenship. This difference in status allowed John Lee to feel a sense of superiority.

For the moment, Uncle Wang was sitting next to

John Lee, dozing. His neck was twisted so that his head faced John Lee, and a scent of cigarette smoke and petrol emanated off him.

John Lee glanced at him, contempt playing across his face. On the stage, a visiting professor of Chinese Studies was delivering a lecture on the quintessence of traditional Chinese culture. It was a topic that interested John Lee, and he listened with some concentration, taking a note from time to time of what was said. The professor launched into a discussion of the Taoist philosopher Master Zhuang, and the extent to which the all-knowing and definitive book which carried his name managed to capture both the spirit of Chinese tradition and the paradoxes of life.

John Lee sat in the audience savouring the moment. Looking around him, he could find nobody he knew. Younger members of the audience had their phones to their ears, with hands over their mouths to hide their smiles. Those slightly older were having difficulty keeping their eyes open, and drifted one by one off to sleep. John Lee turned around and watched as a woman dressed in a coat pulled out a ball of wool from her pocket and began to concentrate on her knitting. He glared at her, but she seemed oblivious to his indignation as whatever shape was emerging from her needles grew in size. It was a child's glove. John Lee turned back and looked at the professor as if apologising to him on the woman's behalf. The professor seemed to understand and smiled at him, as if saying that he didn't mind at all.

The lecture concluded at five p.m., after which the chair of the association summed up briefly, thanking the mainland Chinese speaker in his Taiwanese accent, giving particular emphasis to the word 'mainland'. John Lee heard the sighs of those around him. Uncle Wang opened his eyes and rolled his yellow eyeballs. With his elbow, he nudged John Lee. 'What did he talk about? Was it interesting?'

John Lee bent down, and gave a cough as if to cover his reply: 'Not bad. Worth a listen.'

'I guessed that it wouldn't be much good. Living in New Zealand, what we need is not culture but brute strength.' Uncle Wang rolled up his sleeves, revealing the creases around his biceps.

In truth, John Lee had been excited by what he had heard. He got to his feet and walked over to the buffet table. Wine glass in hand, he looked about, hoping for the chance to speak with the professor – but to his surprise, the professor sought him out first.

'You seemed to be listening very carefully. Are you interested in such things?' he asked.

John Lee nodded: 'I think much of what you had to say is still all too relevant.'

'Indeed. In fact all of the various truths we moderns talk about were known long ago by the ancients. It is just that we ignore what is right in front of our noses, and search in the wrong places for answers. I've read some of the masterpieces of Western philosophy, but I find that they complicate the most simple truths. In this respect, nobody can compare with the wisdom of the ancient Chinese.'

John Lee nodded in agreement. The words of the professor had hit their mark.

'Here's my name card, with my email address,' the professor said. 'If you are interested in talking more about these questions, send me an email.' He placed his wine glass on the table and, smiling, took a name card from his suit pocket and handed it to John Lee with both hands. The card listed his various positions: Professor at the National Studies School of Northern China University, Director of the Research Centre of Traditional Culture and Modern Development, and so on.

John Lee returned home in high spirits. He took out the sirloin steak he had bought several days earlier, marinated it in the red wine he treasured, and set it to fry over a low heat.

Once he had eaten he turned the television to the Chinese news, hoping for a report on the day's lecture. It was not until after ten, when the channel started to broadcast TV dramas, that he relinquished his seat to the woman.

He sat on the bed. He didn't feel at all like going to sleep. He wrapped his feet in a blanket, then draped an oversized brown cardigan around his shoulders. It was his favourite item of clothing, one he had plucked out of a pile of second-hand goods. When he stroked its soft woollen texture he could smell the fresh fragrance of wood. He imagined the former owner of the cardigan – who was sure to have been as elegant and sophisticated as the professor, with a cultivated wife and two lively children, living in a large white house with a tidy garden, two cars, and a small yacht kept stored in the garage.

At midnight, he insisted that the woman come to bed. He turned off the light and reached his hand up underneath her clothes. The room was not heated and his hand was freezing cold; by contrast, her body was warm.

John Lee was shocked at the extent of his arousal. He had thought that he was no longer interested in sex. Over the course of their thirty years together, he had only occasionally made love to her, and then only in the most desultory way. In that moment, though, he felt a sense of movement in his body that had long been dormant.

The rhythm of life in New Zealand was so slow that it seemed to John Lee that time itself occasionally came to a halt. Monday afternoon found him sitting in the shop. Business was falling off by the day. Only a few elderly customers came in anymore, and he had given up trying to talk with them. Over the decade he had been there, whatever topics they had once exchanged words about had been chewed over so thoroughly that they had lost all their flavour.

With the start of May, Auckland's rainy season began; the days were all a dull overcast colour, and the rain came and went, unheralded by wind or lightning, immediately becoming the subject of everyone's attention.

Lying open on the table was a library copy of *The Book of Master Zhuang*, the margins around the philosopher's words filled with scribbled comments.

The woman sat at the door, hugging her water bottle, making a gurgling sound in her throat whenever she took a swig from it, swirling the water around in her mouth before swallowing. She sat with her legs spread wide, and looked uncomfortable, shuffling her thighs, a red welt hidden in the creases of her neck.

Every so often someone would come into the shop and look around, but never with any real intention of buying anything, often just in order to get out of the rain. Now and then John Lee would lift his grey eyes from the book in front of him and glance around in search of them, hoping the customer would leave soon.

It was after three when John Lee received a telephone call from Ye Xiaosheng.

'Uncle Lee,' he said, 'I'm back from Beijing. I've brought quite a few good bits and pieces back with me. Why don't you come over to take a look?'

'Let's wait until the weekend,' John Lee replied, as he marked the calendar with a red circle.

'Beijing's so much more lively than Auckland.

Actually, I'm thinking of moving back there. I shouldn't have listened to my father when he told me to come here. Auckland's going to suffocate me.'

He had bought the shop from Ye Xiaosheng, and anything in his shop worth money had come from the young man, who depended for his livelihood on selling the antiques his father had collected. Ye Xiaosheng's bits and pieces were always good, but they never brought John Lee much of a profit.

'Uncle Lee, when I was in Beijing I discussed a business possibility. I think it has a good chance of succeeding. Let's talk it over when we see each other.'

'You must be joking. With the way things are in the shop, what sort of money do I have for business opportunities?'

'You've been here so long now; you must have a bit put away? It wouldn't take too much money – at first, anyway, and we could take it slowly.'

'Xiaosheng, I have a customer. Let's talk about this on the weekend,' John Lee said, and hung up.

Someone had indeed come into the shop. The footsteps were a woman's, but when John Lee looked up he realised it was truer to say they were those of a girl.

She was wearing a pair of pink sports shoes, her thin legs covered by purplish denim jeans, her grey t-shirt dripping wet, hair draped over her shoulders, her face very pale. She was shivering. A suitcase covered in cartoon stickers stood at her feet.

'Can I stand here for a while to get out of the rain?' she asked in Mandarin, speaking in a low voice.

'Okay,' John Lee grunted, as he pointed at the electric heater. 'Stand over there. It's a bit warmer.'

The girl was like a wounded animal, cowering in the chair beside the counter, not daring to look directly at the woman but stealing the occasional apprehensive glance at her. She was biting down on her lips, showing her white teeth. She hugged herself, her wet t-shirt revealing the contours of her breasts, her collarbone appearing like a necklace around her white neck.

John Lee bent down and turned the heater up, before pouring her a glass of hot water, in an attempt to help her warm up. 'Drink this. It's turned cold today.'

The girl took a small sip of the water, to test its temperature, before holding the cup in both hands to warm them up. Her fingertips were white and woven together like a sliced onion.

'I'm sorry. I'll be off as soon as the rain stops,' she said, looking at John Lee gratefully.

'You can stay until I close up shop,' John Lee replied, standing at the shopfront and looking out at the falling rain. There was no suggestion that it would stop soon. And all of a sudden, John Lee seemed released from his overwhelming sense of boredom.

'Are you travelling?'

'The girl shook her head, a strand of her hair in

her mouth. 'I'm a student here. My lease ended and the landlord sent me packing. I'm off to live at a friend's house.' She spoke so softly that her words were almost swallowed up by the sound of the rain. She removed the strand of hair from her mouth and took a sip of the warm water, moistening her white lips. Her cheeks took on the faintest tinge of pink. She didn't look so pitiable as a moment before; she had now become quite bewitching to him.

The woman, in imitation of the girl, took a drink from her bottle as well, but somewhat too vigorously as the water went straight up her nose. She snorted. Snot and saliva ran down her face as her complexion turned a bright red.

John Lee and the girl both started in surprise. Embarrassed, he wiped the table clean and patted the woman on her back.

'This is my sister,' he said, avoiding eye contact with the girl and pointing at his own head. 'She's a bit crazy, but don't be afraid.'

On Friday, Uncle Wang turned up with some good news.

'My daughter's getting married.'

'Oh, well, congratulations.'

'At the beginning of next month. The banquet will be at Prosperity Restaurant. You're invited,' Uncle Wang said, as he passed over a red wedding invitation embossed in gold.

John Lee opened the envelope to find that only his own name had been printed on it.

Uncle Wang lent closer and pointed at the groom's name. 'James,' he said, 'a young Westerner.'

'Oh, so a Westerner as a son-in-law,' John Lee said, as he checked through an inventory he had been putting together.

'Ha, ha. Yes, that will be an experience.' He cleared his throat. 'I must say that she's doing rather well for herself. She managed to stay on here after her graduation, and now she is going to marry a Westerner. One with a house on the North Shore, as well. He says that we can all move over there once they're married.' Uncle Wang raised his voice, in the hope of evoking some reaction from John Lee.

John Lee seemed unmoved, hiding the envy he felt by wiping down a table that had just been delivered.

'Make sure that you get there early on the day,' Uncle Wang continued. 'I've arranged for association members to have a separate table, and I've invited the chairman to come as well. He's said that he'll be sure to come, and that he'll even sing a song or two to get the party going. Once an opera star always an opera star, you see – he's a born performer.' Uncle Wang stretched out his hand to form 'orchid fingers'.

Sitting at the cash register, the woman suddenly burst into applause, ignorant of the fact that she had not been invited to the banquet. She laughed as Uncle Wang squirmed in embarrassment.

Turning to look at the woman, for a moment Uncle Wang thought he would try to explain to her, but then decided not to. He took his leave.

John Lee patted the woman on her shoulder. 'Nothing I can do about it. None of them want you there.'

The night before they had departed China, as John Lee had helped her pack, he had discovered that the woman owned a violin, all the strings of which had snapped and hung loose from the body of the instrument. The varnish on the finger positions was worn through, evidence of many hours of painstaking practice.

The woman wanted to bring the violin with her to New Zealand, but John Lee had not allowed it, taking it from her grasp and throwing it into a corner. He was determined that she be done with music.

Once all the paperwork for their departure had been approved by the Bureau of Civil Administration, he had gone to her home for dinner. The woman's uncle had replaced his own brother as the district leader; at the dinner, after a glass or two of wine, his face flushed red, he had taken the woman's hand and placed it in John Lee's, saying: 'I give my niece to you; take her as far away as you can. And never come back.'

John Lee was looking awkward in a crumpled dark blue suit. He ate very little but had drunk a lot. Every time a toast was proposed, its aim seemed to be to persuade him never to return to China. He couldn't understand it. He thought that going overseas was something everyone aspired to.

Later on, when he was in the bathroom, he overheard a conversation taking place in a nearby cubicle. 'The little Wang girl is really lucky. As stupid as she is, and yet she's getting married, and going overseas.'

'That Li Yong fellow is an idiot. His woman was fucked stupid by everyone, but he treats her like a princess.'

'I'm not at all sure we have the whole story. What if he knows all that, but he's marrying her just so he can go overseas?'

'I don't think he can possibly know. He was sitting right next to Wang Dazhi, the man who led the charge when his wife was raped. The two of them even toasted one another.'

In shock, John Lee began to shake uncontrollably. It was only with the greatest effort that he managed to settle himself down as he stood there, peeing against the cistern, the arc of his urine sparkling in the moonlight. Shivering, he buttoned his trousers.

He returned to his place at the banquet table. Wang Dazhi, well and truly drunk by now, also returned. A short man, he made a show of patting the woman on the back before turning to John Lee and saying: 'Another toast, my brother?'

Everyone was watching them.

John Lee glanced at the woman. She was trembling

and looked frightened. He was convinced that what he had overheard about her was true.

He stared at Wang Dazhi, his eyes filled with suppressed anger, the glass in his hand at risk of being crushed in his clenched fist.

John Lee could not remember whether or not he drank that glass of wine. He had chosen to forget the moment, just as he had chosen to remember other events. Once the wedding banquet had ended, he was bustled into the bridal chamber, to find the woman cowering in a corner of the bed, her fear plain on her face.

John Lee unbuckled his belt and hurled himself at her, roughly pulling aside her underwear and countering her attempt to escape by holding her down with his elbow, engulfing her in his alcoholic reek.

The woman stopped resisting. She cradled his head in her hands, hoping that once he had pressed his body against her own, he would begin to calm down. Suddenly, John Lee pulled away from her and leapt to his feet. With considerable force, he prised her thighs apart and stared into her depths as if he had seen the light.

After his father died, Ye Xiaosheng had sold his North Shore house and rented an apartment in the centre of the city.

Ye Xiaosheng and his family had arrived in New Zealand even earlier than John Lee had. Ye Daying,

Xiaosheng's father, had once studied connoisseurship with an expert employed by the Palace Museum in Beijing. In 1973, after he had watched this man commit suicide in the moat that surrounds the Forbidden City, he had spared no effort to emigrate to New Zealand, by way of his family connections overseas.

He had departed China with a suitcase full of antiques, many of them treasures that had been seized during the 'Destroy the Four Olds' raids of the Great Proletarian Cultural Revolution and piled up around doorways like so much rubbish. Under cover of darkness, by torchlight, Ye Daying had retrieved these antiques, one by one, thinking he would take them overseas so that one day he might be able to return them to their rightful owners.

When they had first arrived in Auckland, of the three of them only Ye Daying knew any English, so he took a job labouring in a fruit and vegetable shop, turning his hands to all sorts of jobs. Eventually, he had opened up a café of his own. The antiques sat at home and never once did he think of selling them, even in the family's most difficult times.

But their circumstances had never been ideal. First, Xiaosheng's mother sunk into depression and, after struggling on for five years, died. Then Daying developed cancer. His struggle with illness proved even shorter than his wife's; within two years he too was gone. Before he died, he entrusted Xiaosheng with the task of taking the antiques back to China. In his notebook he had kept careful record of where and when he had collected each and every one of them. With a red pen he had marked these places on a map of Beijing, and pinned the map on the wall, so that he would fall asleep each night with his face turned towards it.

Having failed to get into university, Ye Xiaosheng had taken up a job at an insurance company. He proved rather ordinary in his abilities and was forever dependent on help from Chinese friends to make his quota. Once he had sold insurance policies to all the Chinese people in his own circle, he started to venture out in search of new clients. He started joining in the activities of the Chinese Community Hope Association, and found himself, eventually and unexpectedly, elected to the executive. John Lee had come to know him through this connection. Xiaosheng had taken the initiative to introduce himself at one of the association's dinners, addressing him familiarly as 'Uncle Lee'. He enquired about John Lee's background in China, and soon enough discovered some sort of connection between them. He invited him home.

At his home, Ye Xiaosheng took out an insurance policy contract. Close to tears, he pleaded: 'Help me out, Uncle, please. If I don't make my quota I'll be sacked. My dad would die of grief all over again if he heard I was on welfare.'

Xiaosheng sat with the photograph of his father directly behind him and, out of direct eyesight of his father, his crying seemed even more genuine.

John Lee was irritated by Xiaosheng's tears, but from the moment he had come in the door his eyes had been riveted to the small ivory dragon that stood in the book cabinet. He signed the document in a hurry before asking to take a look at the dragon. It was exquisitely carved with a dense pattern of wave-like lines that spread over the creature's body.

'Do you like it, Uncle Lee? It was my father's favourite when he was alive.'

John Lee nodded lightly.

'If you really like it, I'll sell it to you. What do you say to this price?' Xiaosheng asked, and held up three fingers. 'Three hundred dollars. Mate's rates, since we get along so well. My father told me the lowest price I should accept for it was five hundred.'

John Lee patted his trouser pocket. He had just taken some money out of the bank in order to acquire a load of stock that might earn him $200, and now it seemed to be burning a hole in his pocket. He hesitated for a moment and took another look at the dragon. He liked it very much.

'If you really want it, I'll give you a bit more of a discount. Another fifty dollars off. I can't go any lower. Us antique dealers all need a real treasure or two.'

John Lee was tempted, although later on he was to realise that he could have got hold of the ivory dragon for only two hundred dollars. Nonetheless, once he had acquired the dragon he held on to it, placing it in the most prominent position in his shop. He had no intention of parting with it, and whenever a customer asked about the piece he would deter them with an outrageous price.

On the back of selling his father's antiques and one or two large insurance policies, Ye Xiaosheng escaped the rut. He resigned from his job, and set himself up in business.

By all appearances he was a typical Beijinger, his belt loosened to its last eye. From the age of thirty onwards, he had cultivated a scruffy beard that served to hide the scars on his jaw. The scars had been given him by his father; when already diagnosed with terminal cancer, he had discovered that his son had sold one of his antiques, and took to Ye Xiaosheng with a wire-handled feather duster that left deep cuts on his chin.

As John Lee drank the Golden Steed Eyebrows tea that his host had brought back from China, he noticed that Ye Xiaosheng had become even fatter than before. Middle age seemed to have arrived quickly with him.

Ye Xiaosheng brought out a few antiques and placed them in front of John Lee. He did this every time they met, always coming up with some thing or other. Nobody quite knew how large his collection was.

Today, he was happy to offer John Lee a very cheap price. 'Uncle Lee, I can't really get interested in small stuff like this anymore.'

'Oh?'

Ye Xiaosheng moved closer to John Lee. 'This time in Beijing I met up with an official who told me that the best profits were to be made in milk powder. New Zealand milk powder is known by everyone there. Why don't we set up a milk powder brand of our own and export it to China?'

'Huh.'

'Uncle Lee, an opportunity like this, I can't make it happen on my own. I thought of you immediately. You must have put aside a bit in the last few years. And your wife as well. Come up with a bit of money, and you can be the boss and I'll do the work. I've already got things going in China.'

John Lee took a quick sip of tea, scalding his lips. He had been sitting deeply in the sofa, but he now sat up straight, his knees together. Never for a moment had he suspected that Ye Xiaosheng would suggest that they go into business together.

'New Zealand is a hopeless place to make money. Not a bad place to retire, but to make money you've got to go back to China. Just think. There are so many people there, not like here. How much more quickly is the economy growing there? I'm not just thinking about now, but the future too. Are you going to spend the rest of your life living in that old house? Am I going to spend the rest of my life in this apartment?' Ye Xiaosheng spoke with excitement, so that the light caught the saliva at the edges of his mouth. 'I've given the whole thing a lot of thought.

You come up with some money. I'll put some together as well, and I can raise more in China. We'll put your name on the company documentation. That way we can get a bit of a subsidy from the government, since I'm not eligible. At the start we'll need to put as much money in the business as possible, to get things moving.'

John Lee lowered his head and tried to work out in his mind how much money he could pull together. He was shocked when he converted this sum into Chinese yuan in his head. He had no idea how he had managed to save so much. His life wasn't a pleasant one, and he'd never had a day off during his time in New Zealand. Yet his savings seemed like a reward for his hardscrabble life. He could barely believe it, but working it out on his fingers, it was true: he had saved around a hundred thousand New Zealand dollars – five hundred thousand yuan!

Ye Xiaosheng started talking about the profit he expected to make from the scheme, naming figures that John Lee had never imagined he would earn. A tremor of excitement ran through him.

Their conversation became so animated that they failed to hear the voice that came from the bathroom. The door opened a crack, and a small head emerged. 'Xiaosheng, do you have any spare towels?'

The third time that John Lee had seen Jiang Xiaoyu was at Uncle Wang's daughter's wedding reception.

He would never forget their first meeting. She was sitting in his shop, her clothes soaked through, trembling like a wounded animal, biting down on her lips so tightly that they began to bleed. She warmed up a little only when John Lee gave her his coat.

The second time they had encountered each other was at Ye Xiaosheng's house, when she poked her head out of the bathroom door and, not knowing that anyone else had come around, was taken aback at the sight of the two of them sitting together. She blushed, and seemed even more beautiful than when she had sat in his shop.

She soon re-appeared, having put on some clothes, and took a seat opposite John Lee. She hadn't dried her hair, and drops of water trickled down her neck before sliding down between her breasts. She was wearing a pair of pyjamas held up by a cord around her waist. Her exposed skin looked slightly swollen, heightening its delicate texture. As always, she hung her head, reluctant to look anyone in the eye, her stare fixed upon her feet.

'You two know each other?' Ye Xiaosheng asked in surprise, having seen them nod slightly when they recognised each other.

'Uh-huh. I sheltered from the rain in Uncle's shop when I was kicked out by my landlord.'

'You should have told me. I could have come and picked you up from Uncle Lee's shop. He's been helping me all these years.'

John Lee stared at the girl absent-mindedly, not listening to Ye Xiaosheng.

'Uncle Lee, this is my friend Jiang Xiaoyu. She's living here for a while. I'm helping her look for somewhere to live. If any of your friends are letting rooms, do let me know.'

Jiang Xiaoyu raised her head and took a quick look at Ye Xiaosheng, a sense of doubt in her eyes, before hanging her head again. 'Hello Uncle Lee,' she said, her voice thin and reedy to his ears.

He had never imagined that he would meet Jiang Xiaoyu for a third time at the wedding of Uncle Wang's daughter. The unexpected encounter left him even more interested in her than before.

She was dressed in an entirely new outfit. Her blue v-necked sweater showed off her collarbones and accentuated her cleavage. She had her hair tied up, bringing focus to her smooth forehead and pure white neck. She appeared haughty as a swan. She knew no one, however, and as her English was halting, she sat helplessly on her own.

After some deliberation, John Lee struck up a conversation with her.

'Have you found somewhere to live?'

She shook her head. 'I've looked at a couple of places but haven't found anywhere suitable. My old landlord cheated me out of most of my money. Ye Xiaosheng says that he is about to return to China and can't put me up much longer. I don't know anyone here and my English is hopeless. My family used all their savings to get me here. I can't ask them for anything…' Her eyes moistened as she spoke.

John Lee remembered how it had been for him when he first arrived in New Zealand. He too had been in dire straits. On his first encounter with a foreigner, the customs officer, he stammered so badly that he could hardly utter a word. The Maori officer gradually lost patience with him and started gesticulating, asking if he had any illegal products in his possession. Not fully understanding what he had been asked, John Lee stood there rigid. He heard a snort of impatience from the queue behind him, and the woman, who was hanging on to the corner of his jacket in fright, began to panic.

The more nervous he became, the more the immigration officer was convinced that he had something to hide. He was taken off to a small dark room and told to wait until an interpreter arrived.

For the half hour that he sat there, facing the blank wall with the woman's hand in his, it was as if he had fallen into a deep dark valley.

It must be the same for Jiang Xiaoyu, he thought. Faced by her circumstances, she must feel completely at a loss. She always seemed to have her head bowed in fear, never daring to look anyone in the eye.

He thought that he might give her a hand.

'There's a spare room in my house. Why don't you move in for a while?'

John Lee made a habit of reading the newspapers. Once he had a quick glance at the Chinese news and the business advertisements, he would then turn to the second-to-last page to read the death notices of local Chinese people who had recently passed away. His glasses on, he would go through the list name by name, running his finger down the page, in search of anyone that he had known.

He put down the paper and, after waiting for the woman to finish her toast, he pulled her to sit beside him, placing his hand on her knee.

'From today onwards I'm not going to sleep with you. Do you understand?'

The woman nodded her head, breadcrumbs sticking to her lips.

'From today onwards there will be three people living here. The girl is from China as well. I'm sorry for her. She has nowhere else to live. You must make sure not to hurt her or scare her. Do you understand?'

Again, the woman nodded her head, as if she had understood his demands.

He brushed her forehead with his lips, as if to reward her. 'I'm your brother now.'

The woman laughed.

Ye Xiaosheng dropped Jiang Xiaoyu off at John Lee's house. They stood at the front door, and John Lee helped her unload her luggage. She didn't have much, just a pink suitcase and a small bundle of clothes.

'I'll look after Xiaoyu.'

'Yes, I'm sure you will.' Ye Xiaosheng took John Lee aside: 'Uncle Lee. That business proposal we spoke about the other day, have you given it any more thought?'

John Lee had forgotten about it completely, but quickly assumed a serious air. 'Let me think a bit longer. Business dealings, after all, shouldn't be rushed into.'

'That's fine, but let me know about it as soon as possible. I'm going back to China in two days. Give Jiang Xiaoyu whatever help she needs. She's a friend's sister. I'd wanted to look after her myself, but you've seen my apartment. Having her live there was really not appropriate.' Ye Xiaosheng stood at the door. 'I won't come in. We can talk on the phone.'

John Lee let out a sigh of relief. He hadn't wanted Ye Xiaosheng to come inside.

When it wasn't raining, an endless stream of large clouds floated across the Auckland sky, like fairy floss in a child's hand.

In John Lee's imagination, Jiang Xiaoyu had now become that child. He helped her take her suitcase to her room. He had spent the last few days getting the room ready, buying new furniture, putting up pink curtains and buying brand new floral-patterned bedding for her, even polishing the mirror on the wardrobe. She was so beautiful, he thought, that she should spend more time looking at her reflection.

'Is it okay?'

Jiang Xiaoyu sat on the bed, sinking her body into it. Finally, John Lee was given a good look at her face. Her eyes had a tinge of blue in them, and her skin was as flawless as a lily, her lips the colour of the reddest of red flower buds. Without his having noticed her doing so, she had loosened her hair and was now curling it around her fingers in a bewitching manner.

'Uncle Lee, I'm completely satisfied.' She jumped off the bed, and bent over to pick up her bag, giving him a glimpse her breasts as she did so. 'Here's three months' rent. Make sure it's all there.'

John Lee took the money and shoved it into his pocket without counting it. The amount he had asked her for was far less than half what his last tenant had paid.

The woman appeared silently at the doorway, alarming the girl.

'Don't be frightened.' John Lee stood beside the woman and took her hand in his, patting her lightly on the back. 'This is my little sister. She's a bit strange in the head, but she won't do you any harm.'

Once he had settled the girl in he went to bed, half an hour later than usual. Besides reading, he had no other forms of amusement.

During the Cultural Revolution, he had been a librarian, responsible for accompanying the Red Guards on their book raids on other people's houses. The Red Guards would tear the covers off the books and trample them underfoot. Some books would be immediately burnt, others would become targets for criticism meetings. As time went on, John Lee became numbed to everything going on around him, and took to hiding in the office, leafing through whichever books had been fortunate enough to survive the chaos. Once he had read everything to hand, he came across an English–Chinese dictionary in the librarian's drawer. He copied out his first English word. One day, he thought to himself, I will leave this place.

He lay in his bed in the darkness, listening to the sounds coming from the next room. The woman was already asleep and he could hear the steady drone of her snoring. He turned on his side, so that he was facing Jiang Xiaoyu's room. His room was next to her bathroom, and he could hear running water. She was bathing, he guessed. After what must have been half an hour, he heard the sound of her towel as she dried herself, then the opening of a drawer. Now she was patting her body as she stroked her smooth skin. She moved back and forth in the bathroom, her toes drumming on the floor. She pushed open the bathroom door, returned to her bedroom, opened up the wardrobe, and took out some clothes to put on, before sinking loudly into her bed.

John Lee felt himself suddenly inflamed. Had she been naked? He dared not think too much more about that possibility.

She pulled down the bedding and burrowed into her bed, her body now encased in her goose-down doona. She turned back and forth in her bed, as light as a feather. She played with her phone for a while, then put it down, and he heard its chime as it shut down.

After a while the rhythmic sound of breathing came from the next room. She was asleep. But John Lee stayed awake. He stared at the celling. A beam of light from somewhere outside the room had formed a strange pattern above his head.

It was already Saturday by the time Uncle Wang let John Lee know that the annual general meeting of the Chinese Community Hope Association was to be held the following day.

When John Lee complained that he had been told too late, Uncle Wang offered to take Jiang Xiaoyu and the woman to the meeting with him for a bit of fun.

'You don't need to come,' he suggested. 'It'll be boring anyway.'

'That's okay. As it's an AGM, I'd better be there.'

'See you tomorrow then.' Uncle Wang's tone of voice conveyed disappointment.

John Lee rose early to make breakfast. He fried some eggs and bacon, and put a pot of congee on the stove. He placed the woman's bowl and chopsticks to one side, while those of Jiang Xiaoyu he placed opposite his own.

Jiang Xiaoyu didn't get up until nine, by which time he had re-heated the congee twice, carefully scooping off the skin that formed on its surface.

He looked behind him and found her, just out of bed, standing dressed in a pink skirt, over which she had put on a black open-necked cardigan. Her feet were bare and he could see her calves. He was attracted to their round shapeliness; he disliked thin women.

Jiang Xiaoyu covered her mouth with her hand as she stifled a yawn. 'Morning, Uncle.'

'Quick. Take a seat and have some breakfast. I wasn't sure if you preferred Western or Chinese breakfasts, so I've made both.'

Jiang Xiaoyu sat opposite him. She wriggled her thighs, slapping her knees together with a soft thud. She chose a piece of bread and some bacon, and with practiced action started to use her knife and fork. 'Any butter, Uncle?'

John Lee went to the fridge and searched around inside. He could only find a small piece of butter, and he had no idea how long it had been in the fridge. He and the woman never used that sort of stuff. He shook his head, his regret showing on his face.

'Oh. No matter,' Jiang Xiaoyu said, as she lowered her eyes and continued eating in silence.

He felt thrown off balance. Something that every New Zealand fridge should hold was missing from his.

John Lee rubbed the seams of his trousers with his fingers, unsure of how to start the conversation. Breaking a promise, he believed, was a very rude thing to do. 'I'm really sorry, Xiaoyu,' he said, heaving a sigh. 'I'd promised to take you out today for some fun, but I've just found out that I need to attend a meeting. I was only told about it last night. It's an annual meeting. But we'll have lots of chances to go out together.'

'Oh,' she said, hanging her head again. 'Yes, let's think about it later. Your business is important to you.'

John Lee knew she was cross. This silent treatment was clearly how she expressed her displeasure at him for having gone back on his word. Perhaps she appeared so late this morning because she had been deciding on what she would wear to go out with him. He had disappointed her.

John Lee followed the direction of her disappointed stare and looked out the window. Such a fine day. He could see the white rooftops of the houses that lined the shore. The clouds in the sky changed shape endlessly and little boats shuttled back and forth across the harbour. Everything seemed so alive, so vital.

As he came in the door he was handed a piece of paper by the usher with his name written on it. Quickly but absent-mindedly, he took his seat. He had left Jiang Xiaoyu at home with the woman, having first removed all evidence that he and she were husband and wife. Even so, he was anxious that something might have escaped his notice.

He held his mobile phone tightly, his palms sweaty. The phone, which had been given to him by his mobile provider, did nothing but make and receive calls. He had no need for other functions. There was nobody here he wished to be in touch with. But now he sat in fear that the phone would ring and that it would be Jiang Xiaoyu, calling to interrogate him about why he was lying to her. Even worse was the prospect that she might find his deceit so distasteful that she would ignore it altogether.

Uncle Wang sat in the front row. Ye Xiaosheng wasn't there. His flight home had left yesterday. Before he left he had called once more, but John Lee still hadn't come to a decision about the business proposition.

Once the chairman had called the meeting to order, he looked over at John Lee and nodded slightly.

Embarrassed, John Lee forced a smile in return, though the two of them had never exchanged more than five sentences.

In his Taiwanese accent, the chairman recounted the activities of the association over the past year. John Lee had participated in few of them. Only when a lecture topic aroused some specific interest in him would he come along to listen. His mind wandered off, and he thought that once he had helped set up the internet for Jiang Xiaoyu, he might write an email to the Chinese Studies professor, raising various points that had occurred to him in his recent reading of *The Book of Master Zhuang*.

At the end of the chairman's speech John Lee clapped half-heartedly along with everyone else, all the while fixated on the possibility that Jiang Xiaoyu might uncover his deception. Perhaps he should never have tried to deceive her?

All of a sudden he heard his name out loud.

'John Lee.'

He froze.

The person sitting next to him nudged him lightly with his elbow. 'They're speaking to you.'

John Lee stood up, not understanding what was going on. He looked blankly at the chairman; everyone was looking at him.

'John, many congratulations. You have been nominated as an executive officer of the Chinese Community Hope Association.'

A stunned look crossed his face.

One after another, the members of the audience started clapping, beaming in his direction. He was the only new office holder to be nominated at this year's meeting.

'What has been happening?' he turned to the person sitting beside him to ask.

'Didn't they let you know beforehand? You've been nominated for executive office.'

'No,' he stammered out, 'this is a complete surprise.'

Once the voting was over, the chairman invited a

visiting official from the People's Republic of China to address the meeting. This man spoke about China's rapid economic progress, inviting the audience to consider investing in its development. Listed first by the official among items in short supply in China were dairy products. Chinese mothers, he said, are so desperate to get hold of top-quality milk powder that they are quite prepared to smuggle themselves into Hong Kong. The tone of disbelief and disapproval in his voice as he spoke was obvious.

John Lee thought again about Ye Xiaosheng's business proposal.

On account of his new status as an office holder, he decided to stay on for dinner. Everyone who stayed was required to pay five dollars for the meal. As he filled his bowl with rice, the chairman came over to him and patted him on the shoulder. 'John, enjoy the role. Professor Liang made a point of recommending you to me after he spoke to us at our last meeting. He told me of your strong interest in traditional Chinese culture. I hope that you can play a greater part in our meetings, and lend some help to the association.'

John Lee nodded his head, and answered through clenched teeth: 'How come you select new executive officers without first letting them know?'

'I'd asked Mr Wang to let you know. Didn't he tell you?'

In the supermarket John Lee chose the most expensive brand of butter. Having remembered hearing Jiang Xiaoyu say she enjoyed eating seafood, he also bought a fresh fillet of salmon.

Jiang Xiaoyu and the woman were watching television when John Lee arrived home. She was sitting there with one leg stretched out as she painted her toenails a new colour. When she saw him come in the door, she called out: 'Uncle Lee,' and began to fan her foot with her hand so the polish would dry more quickly.

John Lee sniffed the atmosphere to check for any sign of danger. Jiang Xiaoyu seemed intent on the television. She appeared not to have discovered anything.

He sighed with relief, saying as casually as he could: 'At the meeting they insisted on electing me to the executive. I couldn't get out of it.'

Jiang Xiaoyu made a small noise in response.

'They said that I had been recommended by a professor from China. Not someone I know at all well. I have no idea why he suggested me.'

'He probably thinks you're an outstanding person,' Jiang Xiaoyu said, turning her head away to avoid eye contact with him. 'Only someone outstanding is worth recommending.'

'Another thing,' he said. 'Do you remember Uncle Wang? That wedding banquet we both went to was his daughter's. The chairman told me that he had asked him to give me notice of my nomination, but I didn't get anything at all from him.' As he said this, he spread out his hands.

'He was probably jealous of you and didn't want you to know.'

He nodded slightly.

Jiang Xiaoyu cast a glance at him and then looked down again, concentrating on the message she was composing. The waves of her black hair fell over the screen so that he couldn't see the name of the recipient.

John Lee found out the exact time of Ye Xiaosheng's return to Auckland from Jiang Xiaoyu.

He drove to the airport and waited at the arrivals gate. A stream of Chinese faces came through the gate, and for a moment he almost forgot where he was. Thirty years ago, he thought, it was a rare thing to see another yellow face in New Zealand.

He saw Ye Xiaosheng coming out, and hurried to greet him.

'Xiaosheng, I'm here to pick you up. I knew you didn't have your car here and that it would be difficult for you to get home.'

At the car, Ye Xiaosheng crouched down and stuffed himself in through the door. Tapping on the window with his knuckles he said: 'You really should get yourself a new car. They don't even make this model anymore.'

'Yes, yes. I'll get a new one when I have the money. How was it this time back in Beijing?'

'Wonderful. Timing and government policy both seem in our favour,' Ye Xiaosheng said, placing much emphasis on the word 'our' as he cast John Lee a glance. 'A lot of people sought me out to discuss the possibility of working together. And I met several officials responsible for commerce. Now's the time to be setting up in business. Government policy could change before we know it. You should make up your mind as soon as possible.'

John Lee could feel Ye Xiaosheng trying to force him to make a decision. He had intended to tell him that he would go into business with him but, with the words on his lips, he hesitated. He swallowed a mouthful of saliva. 'Let me think a bit more about it.'

Once Jiang Xiaoyu had gone off to class, John Lee went into the woman's room.

He felt that he had been remiss with her in recent days. He hugged her by the shoulders, pressing down on the top of her head with his jaw. He noticed that the grey roots on her head were slowly beginning to take over.

He took her arm and began to scratch it with his fingertips. She loved it when he did this and her eyes narrowed with pleasure, the shallow dimples in her cheeks appeared, and she began to croon softly.

'The last few days have been hard on you,' John

Lee said apologetically, although it seemed as if he was apologising to himself.

He was no longer capable of much physical contact with the woman, no longer able to look directly at the wrinkles on her neck or the phlegm around her lips. Nowadays, there was always a damp spot between her thighs and he suspected that she was no longer fully in control of her bodily functions.

Looking as if he had completed his task, John Lee pushed her away. Flecks of white had peeled off where John Lee had been scratching her arm. Her skin was always dry, like a shell that had been scorched by the coastal sun.

He closed the curtain and hurried her into bed, giving her a glass of water into which he had dissolved sleeping medicine.

He held the key in his hand. John Lee hesitated at the door, then opened Jiang Xiaoyu's bedroom.

The wardrobe door was wide open. It was stuffed with her clothes. He had no idea how she had managed to bring all these clothes with her from China. Clothes in all sorts of colours. As he went over to them, he caught a whiff of Jiang Xiaoyu's sickly sweet perfume. She loved to wear revealing clothes, as if she were trying to seduce the world.

Trembling, he pulled open a drawer. It was full of her underwear, shoved in without any particular order. He couldn't figure out what her style was; half of the pieces had pink flower patterns, the other half were black and lacy and gave off a risqué air. He picked up a pair and held them to his chest. It seemed to him as if the thin material still held the heat of her body and was about to sear his hand.

He felt tired, and sat down on her swivel chair and looked around the room. The bed was unmade, and he could see the traces of her having slept there, the outline of her small body imprinted faintly on the sheets. He wanted to smooth the sheets down but didn't dare, his hands suspended in the air, his fingers tingling as if they could feel what he wanted to touch.

Then he saw the wastepaper bin under her table, and squatted down, like a man searching for a treasure, and carefully went through its contents: several white balls of tissue, some moist cotton make-up pads, a torn receipt. A broken blush compact turned his fingers pink.

He remembered the first days after he had arrived in New Zealand. He had been just as careful then as he was being now, always observing his surroundings. He was afraid of Westerners who came up to him to shake his hand, unsure whether he could trust them.

He was cross with himself for having become too close to Uncle Wang. Plainly he had been made a fool of. He should have made a better show of things than he had at the meeting. He had been unable to say a word, and stood grinning at everybody in embarrassment.

He agreed with Jiang Xiaoyu's using the word 'jealous'

to describe Uncle Wang's attitude to him. To his mind, the wedding had been a farce; the groom's parents hadn't shown up, and thus avoided the torment of seeing their Western son paraded through Chinese wedding customs: short, divorced, all dressed up in a red wedding robe, he had been made to stand on tiptoe to try and catch the apple suspended from a white cord above his head, his nose bumping his bride's again and again until it turned as red as an old drunk's. They had demanded that he drink a toast with Chinese spirits at all ten tables. By the time he had reached the tenth and final table, the Westerner was completely drunk and had begun to vomit. He spewed all over a little girl dressed in pink, and the girl's mother had sworn at him in Chinese. He hadn't understood a word of what was said, of course, and continued to dance around until finally he collapsed on the floor.

But for the fact that he needed to give Uncle Wang some face, he would have burst into laughter. The bride, tall and dressed as always in fishnet stockings and leather hotpants, took hold of her husband and dragged him to a sofa. There, his face was slapped and tea was poured down his throat in the vain hope of reviving him.

Jiang Xiaoyu had sat beside him and laughed her head off like a child.

Jiang Xiaoyu would return home very late each day, always catching the last bus to the stop at the foot of the hill before climbing the slope. Whenever he offered to pick her up she would refuse with a wave of her hand, saying that she didn't want to be a bother to anyone. John Lee admired her sense of independence. They were alike in not wanting to trouble others.

He sat in the darkness waiting for her to return, illuminated dimly by the streetlight shining in through the window.

He heard the front door open, and moistened his lips with his tongue.

'Xiaoyu, you're home?'

He had startled her, and he could hear her heart pounding.

'Uncle Lee, what are you doing sitting here? It's late. Why aren't you in bed?'

He could see her full lips. 'There was something that I wanted to discuss with you.'

'Okay. What is it?' Jiang Xiaoyu said softly, turning on the light and taking a seat.

'No hurry. Why don't you have a cup of water first?' He poured her a cup of hot water and pulled his own chair over beside hers. 'I've been thinking of going into business with Ye Xiaosheng. What do you think?'

John Lee made the story as simple as he could. He had some savings with the woman. The issue was, should he expand his current business, or should he look for new opportunities? Ye Xiaosheng had come up with one, he told her, and wanted him to invest his money back in China. But it had been so long since he was last there and he had no idea of the situation there anymore. He needed her help. 'Xiaoyu, tell me, what are things like in China nowadays?'

Jiang Xiaoyu lowered her voice and waved her phone at him. 'My sister-in-law just rang me, asking me to send her some milk powder. She doesn't trust the quality in China.'

John Lee experienced a sudden flash of understanding.

'The quality of food in New Zealand is world famous. If you can get into the industry, I'm sure the milk powder you export to China will sell well.'

'Mm.' John Lee nodded.

'Rather than buying stuff here for them in a piecemeal way, it's better to export the best products from here to China. All my friends pay a lot of attention to their health nowadays, but if you can't be sure about what you're eating then what's good in theory won't amount to anything.' She stole a glance at him, in case she had said something wrong. 'As long as it doesn't affect your everyday life, then I think an investment like this is a good idea.'

He mulled over what she had said.

'Uncle Lee. I've been talking nonsense, I'm sure. What would a girl like me know? If that's all, I'd better get to bed. I have classes early tomorrow.'

He watched her leave the kitchen, and her words

flowed in his mind. He felt a surge of excitement at the encouragement she had given him, and about the strange new enterprise on which he was about to embark.

He looked at the clock on the oven. Eleven p.m. Most people in Auckland would be asleep by now. He dialled Ye Xiaosheng's number.

John Lee set off early in the morning to withdraw the money. If he combined two of his accounts, he could put together a six-figure sum.

He tapped on the marble counter with his knuckles. 'I'll withdraw the total amount. I don't want to leave anything in either account.'

Jiang Xiaoyu words had proved decisive. She seemed trustworthy, always willing to think about the interests of others.

Ye Xiaosheng was waiting for him at the entrance behind the wheel of a BMW. John Lee squeezed into the car, unconsciously crouching down before realising that this car, unlike his own, was more than large enough for him to sit up in.

He straightened, waiting for the car to start up. Ye Xiaosheng's breath smelt of whiskey. 'Uncle Lee, we've got this. Trust me.'

On the day that they concluded the paperwork for their new business, Auckland had its heaviest rainfall for the year. The wind that whipped up blew so strongly that John Lee's face hurt.

They had agreed to go to China the following month for a scoping trip. It had been ten years since he was last there, and he had no idea what to expect.

Walking around nowadays, you see Chinese faces everywhere. This place has become Chinese. John Lee sighed. How careful he had been, thirty years ago, to try to fit in, to try and become like them.

At the lawyer's office, Ye Xiaosheng took out a box of business cards, already printed with John Lee's name and position on it: John Lee, General Manager, China Dairy Products Company.

He took out one of the business cards and put it into his pocket, thinking to show it to Jiang Xiaoyu when he got home. He thought he might show it to the woman as well, but she would no doubt let out a stupid laugh, without understanding at all the significance of this development.

Ye Xiaosheng dropped him home. On the way, hearing Jiang Xiaoyu's name mentioned, Ye Xiaosheng asked whether she was proving a bother at all. 'She's fine,' John Lee let out. 'She's very sensible.'

'Ah, well, that's good then. I'd worried that a young girl like that might be a bit silly and cause trouble for you.'

Ye Xiaosheng seemed to be aware of John Lee's anxieties, and when they arrived, he did not ask to come in. John Lee hurried up to his house, slipping on the steps made wet by the rain. With some difficulty, he pulled himself back to his feet.

As he turned his key in the lock, he became aware of a burning smell coming from the house.

He rushed indoors in a state of shock. The door to the woman's room was wide open, but nobody was there. Nor was there any trace of her in the kitchen, so he pushed open the door that led into the garden. A patch on the lawn was scorched black, and the air full of smoke. Through it, he saw the woman and Jiang Xiaoyu sitting side by side on the steps, Jiang Xiaoyu's cheeks smudged with black, her eyes brimming with tears. She was patting the woman on her back and trying to get her to cough.

Seeing John Lee, Jiang Xiaoyu's tears finally started flowing down her face. 'Uncle Lee, I'm really sorry. I didn't look after Aunty well enough. A minute ago she just about set the yard on fire.'

Seeing that John Lee had returned home, the woman laughed. Her face, too, was smudged in black.

'What the hell happened?' John Lee asked, trying to keep hold of his emotions.

'I was studying in my room when all of a sudden I smelt something. When I came out to see what was happening, I found Aunty setting fire to a pile of paper. It was already well alight and the grass had caught fire as well. I rushed back into the kitchen to get a bowl of water. It took me half an hour to put the fire out.' Jiang Xiaoyu hung her head again. She had seemed to be apologising for her own mistake, but John Lee knew the fault wasn't hers.

There was no way he could blame the woman, but nor could he go over and comfort Jiang Xiaoyu. He felt that the whole incident came about because he had left the two of them at home on their own. He pursed his lips and tried to comfort them both, the grin fixed on his face even more tragic than if he had been in tears.

Ye Xiaosheng told him their trip to China had been postponed. The specific reasons seemed complicated, and John Lee didn't fully understand them. In short, it seemed it wasn't the right moment for his involvement in the business to be revealed. Some of the contacts they were to rely upon had not yet been confirmed. On the phone, Ye Xiaosheng told him not to worry. Timing was of the essence in business, after all, and as soon as the right opportunity arose, channels would open up to them and the money would flow.

Five of John Lee's business cards had gone from his shop. He found one of them in the rubbish bin when he was emptying out its contents. He picked it out and put it back on the table with the rest.

He was keeping the woman beside him again. She seemed to have been calmer since the fire – which was due to an increase in her medication, he knew, but at the same time he hoped that she had also understood the amount of trouble she had caused, and would become more conscious of her circumstances.

John Lee tried to restore the garden to its former state, but the burnt outline of the fire remained visible on the lawn. He bent over to picked up a discarded cigarette butt and threw it into the bin. He didn't smoke, so the alien object had caught his eye. He took a seat in the garden chair, staring directly at Jiang Xiaoyu's window. He could see a dim light illuminating the room. In his imagination, she would be chewing on her pen and knitting her brow as she concentrated on her studies. He found his own eyes twitching, as if she had infected him with the problem she was working on.

He dug his fingers sharply into his thigh. Then he heard a voice, as if blown on the wind, interrogating him: what point was there to this constant surveillance, to all his imagining? Does she see you how you really are? Can she know what is at work in your heart?

He had no answers to these questions, and started to have trouble sleeping. He would lie in bed gazing up at the high central beam of the ceiling. It was as if Jiang Xiaoyu's eyes appeared there, gazing down on his torment.

John Lee was sensitive to the fact that, since he had become part of the Chinese Community Hope Association's executive, people's attitudes towards him had changed. He was no longer insignificant. On any number of matters, his opinion was now being sought.

He even received intimations that he might aspire to greater things. At the meeting held to celebrate the tenth anniversary of the association, he was seated next to the cultural attaché from the Chinese embassy. She asked him a number of questions, and seemed so impressed by his answers that she told him she would introduce him to the consul general once the meeting was over. After the meeting concluded the promise seemed forgotten, but John Lee smiled at the consul general and nodded his head in greeting, as if to apologise that they had not had the opportunity to speak to one another.

It was no longer Uncle Wang who let him know about association meetings. Now, the secretary of the association would ring him the week before to confirm the time. He, on the other hand, would only ever declare his intention to be at the meeting the night before it was scheduled to take place.

John Lee would occasionally run into Uncle Wang at these meetings, but the frequency of their encounters fell off. He would rise to his feet in anger, then slip back into his chair, a dull look coming over his eyes like two pieces of charcoal that had been extinguished.

He knew that their relationship, never particularly close, had ruptured completely. Once his business with Ye Xiaosheng started to take off, he thought, Uncle Wang will get even more jealous, until his resentment becomes all-consuming.

The evening breeze ruffled John Lee's sparse hair. It was becoming ever more difficult for him to fall asleep, and he would toss and turn all night, trying to suppress the heavy sound of his breathing.

The knock on his bedroom door startled him. In a state of disbelief, he got out of bed, put on his cap, and went to open the door.

Jiang Xiaoyu stood there, cowering. She looked down at her feet. She had given her toenails a fresh coat of red polish. 'Uncle Lee, can you take me into the city? There's something that I need to deal with, and there aren't any buses at this time of night.'

He patted her arm timidly. 'You want to go out at this time of night? Don't you have classes tomorrow?'

She sounded as if she was on the verge of tears. 'It's really urgent. I didn't want to bother you but if I don't go into town my friend will get in trouble.'

Now it was John Lee who was afraid. 'Don't get yourself all worked up. Calm down. Of course I'll help you out.'

Jiang Xiaoyu took out her phone to show him a message. He didn't recognise the number of the sender, but the text read: 'He doesn't want me any more so I don't want to live. I've got a bottle of red wine and sleeping pills. I'm going to end it, Xiaoyu. Look after yourself.'

'This is my best friend in Auckland. I want to go and see her. I have to see her,' she said firmly.

John Lee pulled on his jacket and took his car keys from the table. 'Let's go quickly then. We don't want to be too late.'

The car raced through the streets of Auckland. John Lee ignored the speed limit, feeling quite prepared to receive his first demerit points. Jiang Xiaoyu sat beside him. The tragic look on her face had disappeared, and he discovered that she had put on makeup, her golden eyeshadow brilliant in the darkness. He had never been this close to her. Suppressing his uneasy excitement, he spoke up: 'Your friend won't come to any harm, will she?'

'I don't know.'

'With a friend like you looking out for her, she's very lucky.'

She didn't respond, and they fell back into awkward silence. The streetlights of Auckland seemed arrogant and aloof, each standing on its own corner, refusing to allow its light to mingle with that of the others.

She directed him to a brightly lit street, where she asked him to drop her off. The streets near the house were difficult to access, she told him, but she could walk the rest of the way.

'Are you sure? Should I wait here for you?' he asked, only half believing what she had said.

'No need. I'll stay here tonight. I'll come back once she's settled down.' Her voice took on an anxious edge, and she looked down to check the time on her phone.

John Lee didn't want to let her leave, but he had no alternative. He stared after her as she disappeared from sight at the end of the street.

He was not at all tired. The streets had become busier on a Friday night than they used to be. Shops that would in the past have closed at six were now brilliantly illuminated. As he drove his little lime-green car down the road, the clumsy shapes of young people loomed into sight, and he honked his horn, wishing he could crash into them.

He turned a corner and returned to where he had dropped Jiang Xiaoyu off. It was a bustling street, full of bars, the sound of raucous music and laughter cascading out onto the pavement. The life he had built for himself was so quiet and sedentary that he had forgotten the world contained such rhythms.

Suddenly he thought he could see Jiang Xiaoyu, in a crowded bar, sitting alone with a cigarette between her fingers. She was staring out at the street, her neck stretched up like a proud swan.

He was seized by shock. He must have been mistaken. He stopped the car by the side of the road and walked back to the window of the bar, only to find that the chair he thought he had seen her in was empty. The cushion seat still retained the slightest of indentations, but there was definitely nobody there. He poked his head in the door and looked around. He could see no trace of her. An attractive

Chinese girl greeted him in English, but he waved her away and stumbled back to his car.

'I've really become old. I'm losing my sight.' He was struck by a quite unfamiliar sense of self-doubt.

John Lee helped Jiang Xiaoyu reconnect the internet. He had no need to communicate with the outside world himself. Too much information would cloud his judgement.

Jiang Xiaoyu no longer sat with the woman watching television. She said the internet was faster, but she didn't invite the woman to watch with her. She stayed home the entire week, and John Lee only saw her bloodshot eyes occasionally in the kitchen. She was like a wounded rabbit, wrapping herself up tightly in a blanket and then disappearing.

When she was on the internet, he would read in the room next door, reassured by the sound of her tapping on the keyboard. He had read the copy of *The Book of Master Zhuang* several times, and now he started to take down passages from the book, posting the copied texts on the glass panels in the bathroom, in the hope that she would notice them.

John Lee had used his computer for five years before it gave up, sooner than he had anticipated. He wanted to send the professor an email, and had no alternative but to knock on her door. There were several sentences in *The Book of Master Zhuang* that made no sense to him, and he wanted to ask for help in understanding them.

Jiang Xiaoyu opened the door in her pyjamas, her feet bare on the carpet, her eyes still heavy with sleep.

'Xiaoyu, can I borrow your computer to send an email?'

'Uh-huh. Go ahead.'

She yawned, before getting back into her bed. Soon, she was asleep again.

John Lee looked at her sympathetically. Her shoulders twitched in her sleep, her cheek was pressed against the pillow, hair loose and body relaxed. She looked utterly defenceless.

He typed slowly. In his email to the professor, he wrote about the recent changes to his life. He disliked digital products, and it was as if he could foresee his own future, his shop packed to the rafters with second-hand electronic goods. Lying there, discarded, they resembled white gravestones.

His dislike made him resist these devices with all his heart, and he found he could barely use Jiang Xiaoyu's computer, blundering through its functions until he accidentally opened her photo album.

The girl in the photo album was dressed in the flimsiest of clothes, her face heavily made up, her pose seductive. In one photograph she was in the bath, the white foam concealing her vital parts. Her legs were out of the tub, resting on its side, revealing the delicate soles of her feet.

John Lee looked intently at the girl. Her eyebrows were a little like Jiang Xiaoyu's, but he dismissed the possibility this could be the same person.

'How could it be her?' he asked himself, swivelling around to glance at her on her bed. She was sleeping so sweetly now. He listened to the soft rhythm of her breathing.

He stretched out a hand, thinking to stroke her forehead, as if to make up for his momentary misgivings. His hand froze in the air above her head. He dared not lower it.

After heavy rain, Auckland's winter was fast coming to an end.

John Lee took to rising earlier and earlier in the morning to get breakfast ready, mixing the woman's medicine in her milk and then spending a long time convincing her to drink it. Jiang Xiaoyu went on a trip to the South Island, and the house took on a quiet air again, the rooms echoing with only one set of footsteps.

He renewed his habit of spreading out the newspaper and turning immediately to the death notices to scan the lists for any names he knew.

On his first glance through, he missed the name of Wang Jun, perhaps because it was so common. The second time, however, he noticed the name 'Jim' in brackets, and made an unconscious connection.

It had been more than a month since he had been in contact with Uncle Wang. John Lee tried to remember when they had seen each other last. A couple of weeks earlier he had overheard him speaking with a crowd of middle-aged women at some event or another. They had been laughing at his name. '*John Lee*. Neither Chinese nor European. Only a real alien would take a name like that.' He hadn't bothered to interrupt them and justify himself. He dismissed the incident with a weak laugh and resolved to avoid having anything to do with him in the future.

He stared in alarm at the name in the death notice. He picked up the phone book and found Uncle Wang's number. He had tried to contact Uncle Wang only on rare occasions, and his hand trembled as he entered the number. His heart beat faster. 'Poor old Uncle Wang. Fancy dying so young.'

Nobody picked up at the other end.

His sense of foreboding grew stronger. He dialled the home of the association chairman. It was the first time that he had taken the initiative to contact him.

'Hadn't you heard? Old Wang was murdered by his European son-in-law.'

'How could that be?'

'The newlyweds never got on well. On one occasion, when an argument became heated, Old Wang stepped in to protect his daughter and he hit the husband. The man got drunk and went crazy, and murdered Old Wang. It was all over the news. You didn't see it?'

John Lee slumped back in his chair, holding onto its arms so as not to collapse completely. He could never have imagined Uncle Wang would come to such an end. The details of the man's face were etched in his mind: slightly askew, the stubble on his chin always looking a bit dirty. His mind fixed on the memory of Uncle Wang turning to him arrogantly to declare that he was soon to become a New Zealand citizen.

John Lee's thoughts turned the inevitability of his own mortality. When he had moved to New Zealand, he imagined that he would be able to delay the pace at which death would come upon him. Once he had stumbled by mistake into an Auckland cemetery. The majority of the inscriptions on the gravestones were of people who, he calculated on his fingers, were well over eighty when they died. Thereafter, John Lee had felt quite justified in treating death as an abstraction. Yet he could not forget completely the shock he had experienced upon seeing the death of the director of the library where he had worked. In his last moments, the director's cheeks had flushed an unusual red, and blood had trickled from his trousers, merging with the black of the ink on the books and blurring the patterns on their covers. John Lee knew he avoided the issue of death. He had not returned to China when either of his parents died.

Jiang Xiaoyu rang from the South Island, to say that her trip was to last longer than expected.

John Lee put the receiver down silently. The room was terrifyingly quiet. The woman no longer watched soap operas on the television, and spent her days sleeping instead. When she was awake, she did no more than sit staring at a corner of the room.

He hugged her. 'Why won't you talk with me?' he entreated her.

She remained unmoved. She no longer had that stupid smile on her face and her eyes seemed always anxious.

Her blankness annoyed him, and he dug his fingernails into the palm of her hand in the hope that she would let out a sound. She cried out in pain, but quickly retreated into passivity. It was a long time since he had heard her loud, foolish laugh. Her emaciated body shrank back into the sofa like a coil of rope. The sight of her forced a shiver out of John Lee. He hadn't realised that she had become quite so thin. She had lost entirely the characteristics of womanhood, and her skin had turned a waxy yellow, the wrinkles around her eyes now forming a permanent parabola. She had wrapped herself in a loose pullover she stretched down to cover her knees.

It had been more than a month now that the professor had not responded to his latest email. At the very end of his most recent message, Professor Liang had congratulated him on his decision to go into business. John Lee had wondered whether the questions that he asked might not seem superficial, so he sent the professor a follow-up in explanation. To this, too, he received no reply.

He felt vexed at this lack of basic courtesy. Typical Chinese, he thought to himself. Even if his questions had been naïve, one should have been able to expect some sort of reply, if only out of politeness. To cut off all contact with him, without a word of explanation, was hardly fitting behaviour from a man of such education.

His sense of grievance shook him out of the careful deliberation with which he usually approached life, but there was no one he could complain to.

When John Lee dialled Ye Xiaosheng's number, he heard the voice of a woman standing nearby. The voice fell silent.

'Boss Ye', he said deliberately, 'how's our business going?'

'Uncle Lee, I was just about to get in touch with you. Things are coming together over there. They've received our funds and have begun to put them to work.'

'When can I go and look things over?'

'There's no point trying to hurry the process. The timing's not right. Let's wait until the business has come to something. There'll be time enough for you to worry about it then.'

'Where are you nowadays? I haven't seen you at meetings recently'.

'I'm down in the South Island, working on some things.' Ye Xiaosheng paused. 'I'll be back in two days.

Once I'm back I'll drop by your house. I can't speak any more right now, I'm driving, it's dangerous.'

John Lee hung up. In the thirty years that he had been in New Zealand, he had not yet had an opportunity to go to the South Island. He had heard that it was very beautiful and that it often snowed, but to him all that was just hearsay.

Now he found himself desperate to get down there and have a look around, especially since Jiang Xiaoyu was there. He had no idea what city she was visiting, but he felt sure that he would be able to locate her if he set his mind on it.

His feelings for Jiang Xiaoyu were like the experience of having a finger tattooed: one feels great pain but there is no sign of blood.

John Lee received a telephone call from the association chairman, inviting him over for a chat. Desperate for someone to speak with, he accepted unthinkingly.

The chairman's house was in Parnell, Auckland's richest suburb. The houses there had an air utterly unlike anywhere else, and he recognised the house of the Prime Minister, fringed by a row of pines that made it look like an ancient castle.

The chairman was waiting for him at the front door, dressed in a long linen Chinese robe. He invited John Lee inside. Two hare-lipped white dogs nipped gamely at his heels. He knelt down and scratched them on their stomachs and necks, and they cartwheeled a couple of times in satisfaction before bolting off to the living room. 'Both strays. I got them to keep me company.'

John Lee had never seen a house so large. It was at least three times the size of his own, and decorated throughout in a classical Chinese style. John Lee caught sight of ivory serving maids inset in a yellow rosewood cabinet, surrounded in turn by young serving girls with flower baskets, all exquisitely carved and realistic.

Several scrolls displaying calligraphy hung on the sitting room wall. John Lee couldn't recognise the calligrapher, but could see they were valuable. Pointing at them, the association chairman reeled off the names of several famous artists, before sighing: 'I was given these in the pre-Liberation period. Many of the calligraphers fled to Taiwan. Hard to track them down now.'

He insisted John Lee sit down and have tea, serving him Mountaintop Dragon Well green tea that the chairman had received from back home. As the tea sat brewing, he produced a stack of photograph albums and placed them on John Lee's knee. 'Take a look through these photos of mine. You'll find them very interesting.'

Though John Lee had no desire to pry into private affairs, he started to flick idly through the albums. The photographs were from many years earlier, showing the chairman on the stage. He specialised in playing young female roles, his stature hidden beneath brocade and silk yet giving off a nimble appearance. When John Lee compared the figure in the photograph with the man who now stood in front of him, the contrast was stark, although the chairman's face did retain some of the expressiveness of his youth. He had been short to begin with, and his protruding stomach now served to make him look even more miniature.

After leafing through the albums, John Lee sat with them resting on his knees and looked around at the room. Even at a conservative estimate, the value of the objects surrounding him was far greater than what he would earn in a lifetime's work.

'Why don't I show you around?' the chairman said, before leading John Lee around the house, room after room.

'Here's the guest room. That's an original Zhang Daqian hanging on the wall.' The chairman gave a small nod, tacit permission for John Lee to approach the painting and appreciate its detail.

John Lee moved so close to the painting that his nose was almost touching it. He was trying to fathom the nature of Zhang Daqian's genius. He remembered when he was still in China, and he would ride his bicycle to see exhibitions of this man's paintings. That seemed long ago now. He had been to the art gallery once in Auckland, but found he had no liking for modern Western art. He could never fully understand what it was that the artist was trying to express, and the English-language explanations on the wall always seemed perturbed, angry or obscure. He considered them to be a symptom of the disease of urban affluence.

'This is the audio-visual room. You know I love watching films and listening to opera.' On a large screen on one wall a Kunqu opera was being projected silently. John Lee recognised the chairman in the film, costumed in long pale water sleeves, but had no idea what he could be warbling about.

The chairman was all smiles. He pushed open the door at the very end of the corridor, and they entered an even bigger room, in the middle of which stood a large bed. Two side cabinets of great antiquity conveyed just how much the spirit of Chinese life had changed. A photograph of the chairman as a young man stood on one cabinet, dressed in an immaculate white suit, a pair of round gold-rimmed glasses on his nose. John Lee could hardly believe that the chairman had been so handsome in his youth, like an old-time matinee idol.

'Have you been thinking about old Wang at all? I was told about his death. In China he was an engineer of bridges. I think if he hadn't left, his life would have been easier.'

Uncle Wang had never told John Lee anything about his past life in China. His impression of the man was that he had simply been a long-distance truck driver, who relied on brute strength to make a living.

'When you get to our age, you have no idea when you'll be called to the next life. I'd really like to die in Taiwan, if I can. I'd love to go back. When it comes down to it, this is not my home.'

The chairman patted John Lee on the shoulder. 'Mr Lee. If it's at all possible, I have a favour to ask of you. Once I'm dead, would you take my ashes back to Taiwan for me? I don't have any children. I don't have any relatives. I know that you are someone I can trust. That's why I'm asking this favour of you. I want to be buried in Taiwan. Or my old home in China would do just as well. That way, I'll have someone to speak with once I'm on the other side. I'd be all alone here.'

He was standing in a pool of shadow as he spoke, a gloomy look on his face, as if he had already been shrouded by death.

John Lee felt a cloud of fear pass over him.

From that day onwards, John Lee felt himself enveloped by a dark, vague miasma. He attempted to calm himself down, going to the library to borrow books on Buddhism. He began to chant the prayers they contained. He copied out the chants. It all proved to be no help.

When he checked his phone there were no messages from Jiang Xiaoyu. He had last heard from her three days earlier, when she had confirmed the date for her return as the weekend to come. Over the phone he could hear the tiredness in her voice. He had already started working out how he could mark her return. Like a tiny, exhausted bird, she was returning to him for rest.

Then there had been no news from her. He dared not interrupt her holiday, worrying she'd become annoyed with him. He wanted to eradicate the impression that he was of a different generation to her, so that they might seem to be friends, rather than landlord and tenant.

Since the woman had relinquished her monopoly of the television, it sat unused for a long time. When John Lee touched the ON/OFF button, he found it covered in a thin film of dust.

He turned it on to the Chinese channel. News about the reopening of a seafood restaurant after renovation, and the sale of reduced-price sheepskin cushions rolled on and on. At the bottom of the screen a line of small text appeared: SERIOUS CAR ACCIDENT IN QUEENSTOWN. TOUR BUS OVERTURNED ON THE HIGHWAY. MOST PASSENGERS ARE CHINESE TOURISTS. MANY INJURED.

He felt a knife to his heart. On the phone, Jiang Xiaoyu had said that the last place she planned to visit was Queenstown, and he felt sure she had been travelling on that bus. She would be suffering, and there was nothing he could do to stop it. He changed the channel to TVNZ to watch the live broadcast from the site, scanning the faces of the people being taken off in stretchers to catch a sign of Jiang Xiaoyu. Every young woman looked exactly like her. His eyes streamed with tears.

Three days later, Jiang Xiaoyu arrived home, coming out of the arrivals gate supporting an injured Ye Xiaosheng. John Lee had been early, standing in wait for a long time.

Ye Xiaosheng's leg was bound in plaster, his toes scraping on the ground in a ridiculous animal way.

When he saw John Lee, he forced a smile. 'Uncle Lee, I guess you've seen the news. I was on that bus. Jiang Xiaoyu happened to be in Queenstown as well. She came to the hospital to see me, and then changed her plane ticket so that she could help me come back.'

Jiang Xiaoyu was her usual silent self. She was dressed in a multi-coloured down jacket and wore no makeup. Her manner retained something of the chill of the snowfields.

The three of them sat silently in the car as he drove back into town.

Ye Xiaosheng didn't want to go straight home, saying that he had things to discuss with John Lee, and so he reluctantly pulled up on the slope that led to his house.

Jiang Xiaoyu seemed so tired as to lack the strength to close her bedroom door, leaving it slightly ajar as she got ready to have a bath. Her naked body cast a long thin shadow down the corridor. As the sound of water flowed out the door, John Lee held his body rigid, his limbs becoming stiff with the effort.

'Uncle Lee, things have gone a bit awry with our business venture in China.' Ye Xiaosheng lowered his head, watching for a reaction out of the corner of his eye. 'One link in the supply chain fell through, and the government approvals have taken forever to be issued. They thought we lacked sufficient start-up capital.'

'Oh.'

'So, do you think that you might be able to put a bit more money in? The funds will just sit in the bank account, they won't be used. We just need to impress them. If we don't get the go-ahead, then all that we have done so far will have been wasted.'

'But I don't have any more money.'

'I know. You've stumped up with all the savings that you and Aunty have managed to put together. I won't hide it from you, my trip to the South Island was in search of a possible investor. But I discovered that he moved to Australia some time ago. And now I've ended up out of action.' Ye Xiaosheng was tapping the plaster on his leg. 'I've tried everything I can think of, but we can't rely on borrowing more money. I can't take out a mortgage since I only rent my apartment. Not like you. Here, you have both a house and a wife. I have nothing at all. I'll have to go back to China to start up all over again.'

Ye Xiaosheng said the word 'wife' with considerable deliberation. John Lee's heart skipped a beat, afraid that Jiang Xiaoyu might overhear them. He felt that Ye Xiaosheng was a time bomb, set to go off in front of Jiang Xiaoyu at any moment.

'I don't want to live in my father's shadow. All he wanted out of life was peace and quiet. That's not for me. I've always wanted to succeed. I know that I disappointed him often over the past thirty years. I've achieved nothing. Behind his back, everyone said that he raised a loser. But now I'm going to let him see what I'm made of, really show him he can be proud of his son.' Ye Xiaosheng became more and more worked up as he spoke, and his eyes had begun to well up with tears. But none of this moved John Lee. To his mind, for an adult man to cry in front of anyone else was a disgrace. He needed to get rid of Ye Xiaosheng as soon as possible.

'Okay. Let me think about it a bit more. I'll take you home now. You need to rest after your injury.' John Lee patted Ye Xiaosheng on the shoulder, adding: 'Trust me. I'm sure there's something we can do.'

John Lee walked out of the association chairman's luxurious house, this time with a hefty cheque and a contract in hand. The contract was explicit. Both John Lee's house and his shop were to be used as security for a loan of $600,000, to be paid back within three months, without interest. One condition had not been included in the written contract: on the chairman's death, John Lee would ensure his ashes were returned to China.

He paid a visit to the bank, intentionally picking out a Western teller to deal with. He addressed him in

English, asking him to have the full amount transferred to Ye Xiaosheng's account.

The Westerner took the cheque from him respectfully. An old Chinese woman at the next counter, who was in the midst of depositing her welfare cheque and withdrawing some money, stared over at them with envy.

Very deliberately, John Lee wrote out his own name and the name of their business, China Dairy Products Company, on the form. As he wrote, he visualised the future success of the company, and the possibility that, once things were underway, he'd be able to ask Jiang Xiaoyu to help out with the business and thus see her all the time.

Ten days after the cheque had been deposited, Ye Xiaosheng called from China. Everything's been arranged, he said. The next step would be the search for factory space, and then they could start production. It was a hurried telephone call, and in the background John Lee could hear loud music playing.

He had stopped dosing the woman with medicine; she was no longer capable of causing any great commotion and had become as gentle as a kitten. In a moment of mischievousness, when a group of curious Chinese tourists banged on her bedroom window, wanting to know if anyone was living in the house, she pulled the curtain open a crack and stared back at them. When this succeeded in scaring them away, she clapped her hands in delight.

The one thing he had not anticipated was Jiang Xiaoyu telling him she was going to move out, having successfully applied for a place in university accommodation. Getting to and from classes would be a lot easier for her. She would stay at his place until the end of the month. She had made the announcement at the dining table, her voice as soft and gentle as always, but precise. John Lee had just swallowed a mouthful of bread and he had butter on his lips. His mouth was hanging open but he found he could not utter a word. Her reasoning was indisputable. Even if he offered for her to stay rent-free, he knew she would insist on her decision.

John Lee began to count down the days until Jiang Xiaoyu was to leave. The last time he'd done such a thing was before he came to New Zealand, when the prospect of a new life hung before him.

He took the opportunity of Jiang Xiaoyu being at university to spend an entire day in her bedroom, in something of a daze. He lay down on his side on her bed, counting the strands of her hair on the pillowcase. Long, curly, and raven black: how much he had wanted to find an opportunity to stroke her head.

He rose from the bed and knelt down. He emptied her rubbish bin onto the floor and went through it, item by item, looking for something that could serve as a keepsake of her. He came across contact lenses, pieces of printed paper with numbers scribbled on them, a worn lacy white camisole. He put on his glasses and took a close look at the last item, and after some inspection, noticed a tear in the armpit of the garment. He imagined her embarrassment at finding her breasts had stretched the material beyond its limit. He hugged the camisole to his chest as though it were a prized treasure, and breathed in the smell of her body.

John Lee found it impossible to fall asleep during the last days of her stay with him. He would close his eyes and the image of her face would flood his mind. She was so close to where he was, but only in the darkness could he feel her.

There had been no news from Ye Xiaosheng for fifteen days. The telephone number he'd provided seemed to have been cut off. John Lee began to smell something wrong in the air, but the sensation was always overpowered by Jiang Xiaoyu's fragrance. She had been constantly in his sight over the course of the last few days, bending down to lift bulky possessions, or hanging out her clothes on the clothesline. The sweet smell that emanated from her pores was overwhelming.

The day before she departed, as she had done once before, Jiang Xiaoyu held her up phone to him. 'That friend of mine is playing up again. I'll have to go into the city. She won't give me a moment's peace.'

John Lee drove her into the centre of town, stopping in the same place as last time. She asked to get out. 'Don't worry. I'll be back early tomorrow morning. I still have a few things to pack up.' She patted his shoulder. It was the first time that she had touched him of her own accord. His legs trembled and, in the dim light of the street, his throat quivered.

She stood under the streetlight and watched him drive away, before turning around and disappearing into the surrounding darkness.

But John Lee hadn't left. Stopping the car not far away, he emptied his pocket of coins and paid them into a parking meter. Enough to last the night. He didn't want to go back to the house. With her gone, the house no longer had any meaning.

He traced her footsteps and found himself once again in the narrow lane. He began to tread softly. He wasn't tailing her; he felt this deep down, but also knew he was unable to stop.

Jiang Xiaoyu had entered an apartment block, punching a pin number into the security panel at the entrance. The door sprung open and she slipped in, pressing the button for the sixteenth floor.

The apartment block must have a side entrance, he thought. He set off to walk around it. Sure enough, he came across a small entrance where the rubbish bins were lined up. The door was not locked. He went in and pressed 16.

He got an odd feeling as soon as the lift door opened. He had been here before. The voice-activated hall light flicked off. He dared not take another step. The place seemed so familiar.

From a door marked 16B John Lee heard the sound of a voice he knew.

'All packed up? See you back here tomorrow?'

'Um. You've set everything up over there?'

'The money's in the account. Enough for us to leave for Australia.'

'That old man hasn't managed to get hold of you, has he? I'm just a bit worried we've gone too far.'

'Baby, don't stress about it.' John Lee heard Ye Xiaosheng kiss Jiang Xiaoyu on her cheek, and imagined the rasp of the man's stubble on her soft skin. 'They'll get along fine. They're survivors. Otherwise, they wouldn't have kept things together in New Zealand for so many years. Anyway, whenever I remember how he was looking at you all the time, I think that we deserve his money.'

'I wouldn't have been able to put up with him if you weren't here.'

He heard the sound of a cigarette lighter. With the greed of an addict, Jiang Xiaoyu took a suck or two on the cigarette before passing it to Ye Xiaosheng.

'You know, honey, our success is entirely down to you. And you didn't suffer any harm. Old men like him might well have evil intentions, but they don't have the courage to put them into action. In any case, that imbecile of a woman was there all the time keeping her eye on him.'

'And after all that, he didn't even tell me she was his wife.'

'Exactly. That's why I say that he was trying to cheat us as much as we've cheated him. Don't worry about it. I've taken care of the whole thing. I've been talking with a lawyer. Just blame it on a box of business cards he took for genuine.'

John Lee had edged closer, and he could hear through the thin door so clearly that the tremor in their voices, the sound of their lips meeting, the smack of their kisses all reached him. These sounds were soon followed by moans from Jiang Xiaoyu, and, as he had so often heard in his own house, the rustle of her clothes dropping to the floor.

Something deep within him that had come back to life was slowly dying once more. The blood in his veins began to dry up, and the intervals between the beats of his heart lengthened, but each beat now seemed to strike at his chest with the force of a hammer intent on shattering it.

It was afternoon before Jiang Xiaoyu returned to the house.

John Lee had not slept. He averted his face from her, not wanting to show his bloodshot eyes.

The woman was still asleep, snoring loudly. John Lee busied himself in the kitchen. He had rushed off to the supermarket as soon as it opened, and filled up the boot of his car with groceries as if bringing home provisions would calm him down.

Jiang Xiaoyu was walking restlessly about the house, and the rate at which he chopped the vegetables kept pace with her footsteps. He stayed quiet, but out of the corner of his eye caught sight of a red mark on her neck.

He cooked her favourite meal: pan-fried salmon, adding extra butter and lemon to the recipe. The salmon steaks changed colour in the pan, and even when hot oil spattered onto his hand, he hardly noticed it.

He set the table for three, the reflection of his exhausted face distorting in the silver cutlery. He filled three glasses with red wine and, with his back turned away from her, dropped the white medicine into the furthest glass, agitating it so the powder dissolved.

'Xiaoyu, you're leaving tomorrow. Uncle's cooked you a farewell banquet.' He placed the glass in front of her.

He picked up his own glass, and placed the third in the woman's hand. 'We wish you success in the future. Our time all together has been a happy one, hasn't it?'

Jiang Xiaoyu's face was flushed red, as it had been the first time they met. She hung her head as low as possible.

'A toast. How fortunate that we should have met here in New Zealand.' The three of them clinked their glasses. 'It was destiny that brought us together.'

They took a long time eating. Once, John Lee tested out Ye Xiaosheng's name, and watched a flash of anxiety pass across her eyes before she changed the subject. He left it at that.

The woman was covered in fermented bean curd she had been trying to spread on a piece of bread, and John Lee gently helped her wipe her hands clean. He had never been so solicitous of her in front of Jiang Xiaoyu.

Once the meal was over, Jiang Xiaoyu offered to help him dry the dishes. He washed with painstaking care, watching the indistinct reflections of the two of them in the wet plates. As he stacked them up, he decided that he would give her another chance. Surely she didn't intentionally lie to him.

'Let's go out into the garden to sit for a while.' Having finished washing the last plate, he rinsed his hands in cold water to wake himself up.

Though several months had passed, the smell of burnt grass lingered. John Lee took a seat in the wooden chair and removed a pack of cigarettes from his pocket. He offered one to Jiang Xiaoyu. 'A cigarette?'

Jiang Xiaoyu hesitated, before hanging her head again. 'Uncle, I don't smoke.'

'Oh.' He put the packet back in his pocket. 'Ye Xiaosheng left them here. I thought you smoked.'

In the darkness he saw her fingers twisting the material across her knees. He held up the cigarette lighter and struck it, looking intently at the expression it illuminated on her face. She was as beautiful as ever. He would remember forever the first time he saw her, soaked to the skin and trembling. At that moment, he had wanted to hold her in his arms and stroke her shoulders, to say to her: 'Don't be scared. Now that you're here in New Zealand, everything will get better. Trust me.'

Jiang Xiaoyu was lost in thought, gazing at her feet as she swayed her legs. The green of the lawn stretched all the way to the foot of the mountain. In the distance the flashing lights of Auckland's Sky Tower were suspended in space. The occasional sounding of a ship's horn interrupted their awkward silence.

The wind had risen, and the night had turned cold. Jiang Xiaoyu hugged herself, yawned once, and said: 'Uncle Lee, I'm off to bed. I'll be leaving early tomorrow.'

'Sure.' John Lee stared at the far-off lights. Reflected in his eyes, their various colours merged into a single red tone.

John Lee looked at the time. He had worn his wristwatch, a 1970s model, for more than a decade now. It had marked his passage through time without ever making a mistake.

Eleven p.m. By now, he thought, the medicine would have done its work. He had showered, scrubbing his entire body so that the smell of soap emanated from every pore.

John Lee put on his favourite cardigan, combed his hair in the mirror, ruffled it and then flattened it with his cap. He forced himself to stand up straight, pulling in his stomach and pushing back his shoulders, as if he was seeing himself thirty years ago.

He put on his woven calfskin shoes, his best pair. He had made a point of polishing them this morning, and placed them out in the garden beneath Jiang Xiaoyu's underwear on the clothesline, which she had not had time to collect, and which swayed like flowers in the wind.

John Lee pushed open his bedroom door and followed the dim corridor until he reached her door. He tapped softly with his knuckles, but there was no response. Without hesitation and with a smile on his face, he turned the handle and pushed the door open, leaving it slightly ajar behind him. In the half-light of the bedroom he could see Jiang Xiaoyu lying on her bed. She had fallen asleep in her clothes.

Now, finally, he found the courage to envelop her body with his hands. Her exposed skin was so smooth, the texture of silk. His hands roved up and down her, like a child trying out a slide.

Jiang Xiaoyu stirred but showed no sign of waking. He felt emboldened, and bent over and lightly kissed her forehead. He covered the red mark on her neck with his hands, wanting nothing to ruin his impression of complete beauty.

John Lee tugged on her shoulders so that she lay flat on her bed, making it easier for him to remove her clothes. One by one he undid her buttons, with the deliberation of someone engaged in a solemn ritual.

Every button was undone. He could see her black lace panties, sexy and mysterious. His hand followed the line of fabric and pushed its way underneath. He stroked her with the care of a man seeking a treasure.

He felt the blood pulsing through his body. He was as hard as iron. He tried to control himself, to slow things down, in case it all happened too quickly.

'Why did you try to cheat me? I've always liked you. You must have known that.' He took his hand out of her underwear and brushed it over her face, stopping at her lips as if he was afraid of the answer.

'Why did you leave me with nothing?' John Lee bent over and pressed his lips to her face, kissing her all over. It had been a long time since he had had a proper kiss, and now he seemed clumsy and out of practice. Slowly, Jiang Xiaoyu's eyes began to open. Seeing John Lee on top of her, she pushed as hard as she could to get him off her. He clamped onto her wrists. She began kicking frantically with her feet. He pressed down on her thighs with his knees, rendering her still.

He kissed her, his saliva moistening her cheeks, and as his lips ran across her face, he heard her shout, 'Let me go!' He paid no attention. He was beyond pity.

He could feel her tears. She was a small creature, bound up tight but pointlessly trying to break free. He no longer trusted her and forced himself to continue, like a hunter would.

He pushed her bra upwards, exposing her breasts. Their fullness forced him to think of the woman's shrunken flesh. Having no desire to see her emaciated body, he had grown used to making love with the lights out.

He bit down on her nipples like a murderous warrior, and Jiang Xiaoyu let out a scream of pain. Unmoved, he became even rougher. His fingers forced their way inside her, against all resistance.

He wanted to tear her apart, but nothing could stitch up the wound he had suffered at her hands.

The sound of the television in the living room was getting louder and louder, and the warped dialogue of the old opera that came to him kept him from distinguishing the sounds of the real world. He had nothing to his name now, and no fear that anyone could take something from him.

A noise came from the corridor, muffled by the carpet.

The door opened a crack, letting in a beam of light, followed by a shadow.

Jiang Xiaoyu's eyes were wide open, staring at whatever was behind him. She seemed about to say something, but he covered her mouth. Both of their lips had been bitten, and blood covered their teeth. He could taste her saltiness.

She raised her feet and kicked out. She had pulled his cap off his head, his greying hair gelled in place. He had no time to pick up the cap, but forced his body to become even harder.

In the dim light of the bedroom, the shadow fell onto the wall, faintly.

Jiang Xiaoyu had stopped resisting. Her eyes were wide with terror. She was at last scared of him, John Lee thought, at last experiencing fear, and this was the cost of her deception. The thought inspired pity in him once more, her wide eyes softening him. With one hand still stopping her mouth, he supported her body with his other hand so he could slow himself down a bit.

John Lee began to enjoy the activity, and the expression on his face relaxed. His eyes narrowed in pleasure. Looking at the girl beneath him, so soft and smooth, he felt protective of her once more.

Somewhere behind him, there was a sudden, ugly thud.

His movements slowed, his strength left him, and his anger and resentment flowed out of the new wound.

He slowly turned his head and saw the woman, a broken red wine bottle in her hand. Her face was fixed in an expression of alarm and she was trembling, her eyes wide open.

It was the expression she had on her face thirty years ago when he had forced himself on her; with her fingernails digging into his back he had ignored the pain and pushed on further. He tried to avoid looking at her, but the terror that flashed in her eyes was imprinted on his mind. They were like two captured animals fighting to the death.

The red wine dripped onto the carpet and formed a puddle.

The woman shrank back into a corner of the room and curled up, her head cushioned in her right arm, the fingers of her left hand scratching at the wall, boring their way into the plaster, gathering a film of white fragments. She stuffed her trembling fingers into her mouth like a child who had done something bad.

Jiang Xiaoyu lay spread out on the bed, naked, staring helplessly at the ceiling, tears flowing silently from her left eye.

John Lee felt around to the back of his head with his hand. He could not tell what was blood and what was wine.

All he could feel was that he was sinking.

Duncan M. Campbell is a New Zealander who has taught modern and classical Chinese language, literature and history at the University of Auckland, Victoria University of Wellington and Australian National University. His research concentrates on the literary and material culture of late imperial China. In 2015 and 2016 he was Curator of the Chinese Garden at the Huntington Library in San Marino, USA.

Huo Yan was the recipient of the Rewi Alley Fellowship at the Michael King Writers Centre, Auckland, in 2013. *Dry Milk* was written as a result of this residency.

This translation was commissioned jointly by the New Zealand China Friendship Society and Victoria University of Wellington's Confucius Institute. Duncan M. Campbell thanks George Andrews and Luo Hui for their support.

The Giramondo Publishing Company acknowledges the support of Western Sydney University in the implementation of its book publishing program.